The year is 1651 and England's only hope for the future lies in Charles Stuart's escape to France from Cromwell's rule. To Verity Ashbourne, a secret follower of the King, the advent of Richard Kingston, the commander of a troop of Roundheads billeted at her home, is a continuing threat to that hope and to those of all royalists.

How can she remain silent when she suspects him of being a spy? Yet any other time but this she might have loved such a man . . . She despises all he stands for, so why does her heart play the traitor?

King's Puritan

Jean Evans

MILLS & BOON LIMITED
London · Sydney · Toronto

First published in Great Britain 1982
by Mills & Boon Limited, 15-16 Brook's Mews,
London W1A 1DR

© Jean Evans 1982
Australian copyright 1982
Philippine copyright 1982

ISBN 0 263 73786 1

Set in 11 on 11½ pt Times

Photoset by Rowland Phototypesetting Ltd
Bury St Edmunds, Suffolk
Made and printed in Great Britain by
Cox & Wyman Ltd, Reading

CHAPTER
ONE

THE October sun had vanished, leaving the sheltered cove a suddenly alien place. Unnoticed by the solitary walker the sea had changed within the space of minutes from blue to a turmoil of pewter grey as a keen wind whipped in across the land.

Verity Ashbourne had known the sea all her life, knew it well enough to respect its changing moods, but today her mind was elsewhere. She shivered, casting a half anxious glance at the sky, but she had no wish to return to the house just yet, knowing her aunt's mood. Even thinking of it was sufficient to make her tremble and she wrapped her arms about her in a self protecting embrace. If only she need never go back!

She bent to scoop a handful of water from a pool in order to cool her cheeks and saw an image of wide eyes in a face framed by wind-swept hair reflected back at her. She drew away. Her aunt spoke often of the evils of vanity. The air had grown cooler. Gulls screeched voraciously along the changing water line, driving and wheeling, retreating before the force of the tide. With a slight feeling of alarm she saw the thin veil of mist beginning to creep over the water. Soon she would have to return, but, for the moment, freedom was sweet.

Fine shingle grated and hollowed under her feet as, gasping against the cold wind, she walked on blindly. It would be dark soon. Within minutes the mist had thickened and was rolling in towards the land. Then her gaze was held frozen as she stared out to sea. For one brief moment she had imagined she saw a ship out there, its hulk visible for only a second before it vanished again. She tried to pierce the gloom, walking towards the water's edge, but there was nothing to be seen and she frowned. She had been so sure. Ships frequently did travel this way to the Cinque Ports of Rye and Winchelsea, vessels bearing the emblem of Cromwell's navy, but few came in so close to this stretch of the shore unless they had reason to wish to evade the ports. She had heard the stories of illicit trading that went on along the coast, of the mysterious figures who slipped ashore, perhaps at Dymchurch or Rye, with cargoes of brandy or wine or fine Brussels lace.

Her heart beat a little faster. Was that what she had seen? A vessel waiting for cover of darkness? She searched the gloom, but nothing stirred the muffled stillness. She began to feel uneasy at the idea of finding herself an unwilling witness, and became aware with a new sense of alarm that, while she had been so absorbed in her thoughts, the tide had crept up unnoticed.

To her horror she saw the sea lapping gently over the stretch of shore on which she had walked. The tide, tugging at the shingle, brought with it the smell of weed and salt. A quick glance behind her showed the steep rise to the cliff top. She had walked much further than she had imagined. Scrambling over the ridge of shingle she tried to climb hurriedly upwards, only to be hampered by her skirts and the crumbling earth. She clutched wildly at clumps of sparse grass, but it was no good, they slid through her hands. With a sharp exclamation of dismay she abandoned the attempt. She would make no progress this way.

She stared uneasily at the rapidly encroaching tide. If she remained here very soon she would be cut off completely and would drown. She couldn't climb. There was only one way, if it wasn't already too late.

Gasping at the iciness of the water, she held up her skirts and waded into it, shivering as much from fear as from the numbing chill of the wind. If she could only make her way round the small outcrop of rocks the tide would not have reached the far cove yet. From there she could reach safety.

But already the sea was lapping at her legs. Her skirts were billowing, dragging her away from the precious holds in the rock surface. Her fingers were almost too numb to feel the crevices any longer and the mist seemed to be pressing in upon her like a suffocating grey blanket.

Then she heard the sound, a steady thud, again and again, nearer and nearer. Instinctively she froze, listening, trying to pinpoint the direction of the sound. Then, out of the mists something came. Her mouth opened to cry out, then the shape of an oar rose and fell. A wave surged up to grip her, tearing her away from the cliff and, as she fell, something struck her a violent blow.

Dimly she was aware of the voice, startled, angry, somewhere above her, before the water closed over her head, filling her mouth and nose, choking her as she fought, gasping for the surface. Her lungs felt as if they were bursting.

Hands reached down. 'What the devil . . .' She was caught clumsily and lifted bodily to find herself lying, choking, in a small rowing boat. A man's face loomed above her, the features hard as he bent to push the tendrils of auburn hair from her face to study her more closely. Where had he come from?

She was conscious of fingers fumbling at her bodice and tried to cry out in protest, but the sound was lost as her throat tightened in a spasm of terror. A hand moved against her naked flesh and was pressed against her heart. She couldn't move, her entire body seemed to be gripped by exhaustion and numbness, then she was shaken roughly and something was poured between her lips, leaving her gasping as the spirit burned.

'Come on, my little mermaid, breathe. Breathe,' the voice commanded. She tried, angrily, to thrust him away as he shook her. A protest rose only to be silenced by the hand he clamped roughly over her mouth. 'Aye, that's better, but quiet. Breathe by all means, but don't make a noise if you know what's good for you.' His voice was a grim whisper. She fought, her heart beating wildly, and his hand tightened, warningly. She had to have air, her senses were reeling. She nodded and mercifully the pressure relaxed.

'I will be quiet.' She gulped in fresh air gratefully, quivering in every limb. She was aware that he had straightened up and seemed to be listening for something. Her own ears heard nothing but the racing of her own pulse and the sound of the waves slapping gently against the boat.

Huddled, shivering, in the bottom of the boat, she had time to study him. His hands were tanned and strong, but it was his face which held her. His nose was straight, the mouth arrogant, yet with a sensuality about it which promised gentleness, and at the same time a hint of cruelty. A rivulet of sweat ran from his brow, darkening the lock of hair which had fallen forward. But his eyes . . . a faint tremor ran through her then as she became aware of his dark gaze turned with mocking amusement upon her own curiosity. She hadn't realised she had been staring. He moved and shadows flitted across his face so that she could no longer see him clearly. She shivered. Who was he? What business brought a man out as darkness approached, and in a small craft like this? Was he a smuggler? She was glad he couldn't see her own expression as the colour drained from her cheeks. If he was there was no evidence of it. Then she remembered the ship, the one she had thought to be a trick of her imagination. This man, by his dress, was no fisherman. He must have come from somewhere.

She stirred and tried to sit up as the warmth returned to her limbs and his gaze went swiftly to her.

'Lie still,' he rapped softly, yet leaving her in no doubt that if she disobeyed he would not hesitate to enforce her obedience.

Her hands clutched nervously at the sides of the boat as he manoeuvred it expertly from a spot where the current surged against the rocks then, after a moment, he spoke again, watching her intently.

'For a mermaid you don't swim too well.' Laughter touched his dark eyes. 'What were you doing in the water?'

She blushed, glad of the darkness which hid her confusion. 'If it is of any concern to you, I was escaping.'

She heard his soft laughter. 'Why, what have you done?'

She bit her lip, turning her head away. 'It isn't what I've done, so much as what I have left undone.'

'I see, and is that sufficiently serious that you must run away?'

'If you knew my aunt you might think so,' she responded, and heard him laugh aloud.

'Then I'm glad to have missed that pleasure. The question still remains, however, of what is to be done with you.' He was silent and she tried to read his features in the darkness, sensing that his mood had changed.

'Where are you taking me?' Her eyes scanned the inky depths of the water.

For a moment he concentrated solely on his task before his gaze returned to her, flicking with amused curiosity over her body in the clinging wet gown. Her hand rose to her throat involuntarily as she realised for the first time how she must look.

'If you were truly a mermaid I'd drop you over the side and let you swim. Alas, I think you must be mortal after all, or perhaps there are even mermaids who never learn how to swim. Which are you?' A pulse hammered in her throat and his lips curved, mockingly. 'Human, yes, very definitely. Unfortunately, that makes you all the more dangerous.' His interest seemed to be diverted then, as he scanned the rise of the cliff. There was something about him which intrigued yet at the same time filled her with apprehension.

'I shall put you ashore somewhere.' The dark, unfathomable gaze was turned to her again. 'And I would suggest that you get out of those wet things when you get home.'

Relief flickered through her. She had not felt

consciously afraid of him, strangely enough, yet now he made her suddenly aware of her own vulnerability.

'I owe you my life, Sir. I would thank you if I knew your name.'

It was as if a shutter came down between them and she sensed his sudden withdrawal. 'Save your thanks, Mistress. I want nothing from you but your word.'

Her eyes widened. 'My . . . word?'

'Is it too much to ask?'

She frowned. 'I am not sure what it is precisely that you ask. Why should my word matter?'

He gave his attention to the oars and made no answer, then the boat jarred against shingle. She didn't move, indeed, she felt incapable of movement. Without a word he leapt ashore and, as she hesitated, he reached down for her, lifting her with ease. She expected to be set down on her feet, but instead he held her, looking down into her face. Colour stole up into her cheeks at the intensity of his gaze. No man had ever looked at her in such a way before and her heart began to beat unsteadily. She trembled as she became aware of the warm, muscular strength of his body against her own, but as she moved, half protesting, his grip only became firmer.

'Well, Mistress, I want your word that you will say nothing of having seen me. I saved your life, now I ask this in return.'

She drew in a breath, her hand against his chest. 'Pray, put me down Sir, I am well able to walk.' It was untrue, she discovered to her humiliation, as he lowered her and she swayed. In an instant he was holding her close and some expression stole into his eyes, an expression so disturbing that she stayed within the circle of his arms, conscious of his closeness and the strange effect it was having upon her senses.

'I find myself very reluctant to let you go,' he breathed, softly. 'Were it not that you would undoubtedly catch your death of a chill and I have other business, I might not be persuaded . . .' Even as he spoke his lips moved against her hair, her neck, then his mouth possessed hers. Her senses reeled as she became horrified by her own traitorous feelings. She moaned softly and broke away.

'Why should I give you any such promise?'

'You owe me your life,' he said, softly. 'If we should ever meet again fate may well make you the keeper of mine.'

Her mouth was too dry to make any answer and before she could recover he had pushed the boat away, leaving her standing alone on the shore. Within seconds he was swallowed up in the mist and she stared into the darkness, her arms hugged about her. It was as if he had never existed, except that her mouth still seemed to feel the pressure of his lips burning upon hers. Her mind was in turmoil. How was it possible that they should ever meet again, and if they did, and it should prove her duty to tell what she knew, would she do it? Something within her rebelled at the thought.

Darkness had come swiftly, yet even now she felt reluctant to return to the house. She pressed a hand to her cheek, feeling it burn, and she thought with horror of what her aunt would do if she ever discovered what had happened. And yet, Verity closed her eyes, how could she hope to conceal the strange new emotions which had suddenly been stirred up within her to course like a flame through her body, bringing with it a frightening new awareness.

She began to run, as much from her own thoughts as from the knowledge that her absence would have been noticed, and her aunt would be furious because she had spent her time with grandfather instead of completing the tasks she had been given to do.

The wet gown flapped against her ankles and she shivered. Her heels caught in the rough cobbles of the narrow street, but she was hardly aware of stumbling. Her nostrils caught the faint tang of salt coming with the wind from the Marshes, those two-score miles of desolate, mist-shrouded wastes across which few men ventured. She felt no fear of them, nor of the sea. It was an inexorable part of her life, all about her. To the east the cliffs running beyond Hythe and down to Dymchurch Wall. Rye, with its cobbled streets and the Mermaid Inn, and a church, now in a ruinous state. In the reign of Elizabeth the men of Rye had put five ships to sea against the great Armada and had been rewarded by the gift of six great cannon.

Her breath rasped in the air as she ran. Already lamps were lit in the cottages, casting a pale glow upon the occupants who went about their own business, paying no heed to the running figure. Trade erupted noisily from the Blue Boar Inn onto the street. She side-stepped the brawling figures, drawing her cloak more securely about her.

Kingswood stood back from the cliff top. The shutters had not yet been closed so that she could see the lights from the lamps glowing in the distance as she raised the hem of her skirts and sped over the grass. Nearly two centuries had mellowed the brick and timbers of a house built by generations of Ashbournes. Those years had seen the ivy spread from crack to crevice until it covered the walls, obscuring the family crest.

Verity remembered her father's pride in this house, a pride which, from the moment of her birth, he had instilled into her, and a rare feeling of anger seized her now as she crossed the terraced lawns and saw shadows cast across neglected rose beds and hedges, the secret arbours where, as a child, she had played. How her father would hate to see what it had become.

She passed beneath the stone arch of the gatehouse and reached the servants' door, letting herself in quietly before making her way stealthily towards the stairs. She stood, shivering, in the darkened hall, aware of the library door which was cracked open, halting her flight to safety. Her breath came in painful gasps as she drew back into the shadows cast by the great log fire.

At first she was only half aware of the voices which came from behind that door, her cousin Prudence's, raised, angry, her aunt's, reassuring. Only gradually did the sense of what they were saying begin to penetrate her brain and she stood stock still, listening yet scarcely believing.

'Why should my cousin have everything? It is so unfair. Surely we have as great a right . . .'

Verity heard her cousin stamp her foot and her mind conjured up a vivid picture of Prudence's pretty face, distorted as it so often was by sullen anger.

'You foolish child. Will you ruin everything for want of a little patience?' she heard her aunt say.

'Your grandfather is old and sick. He cannot live for ever.'

'Nor can I wait for ever. I hate him.' Prudence wept bitterly, and it was all Verity could do to stifle a gasp of horror. She knew she should make her presence known, yet something held her back, as if she must be certain that what she heard was real. 'I hate him and I hate his charity,' Prudence cried.

'And I tell you it will not be for much longer,' her aunt said, sharply. 'And when he is gone we shall have everything.'

'You forget, my cousin is still his heir. It was her father who had the fortune to be born the eldest son, not mine. Nor is he likely to forget that mine chose other loyalties.'

Verity heard the sound of a sharp slap and Prudence wailed.

'I will have no such wicked talk,' her aunt said. 'Must I remind you that Charles Stuart is on the run, a declared traitor? He may call himself King, but he will never wear the crown and there will be no place in England soon for royalists. Your cousin will learn then what it is to be the pensioner, *our* pensioner.'

Verity fled blindly before the sound of their laughter. Gaining her room she stood for a moment leaning against the door, breathing in deep gulps of air as she tried to still the tears. For once she was grateful that Margaret, her old nurse, was not there to see her as her image was reflected back at her from the glass, her eyes bearing the look of a hunted animal. She had never imagined that such hatred could have been nurtured over the years by her aunt and cousin, and it stunned her now. Far better if she had drowned than face a future so bleak. The stranger had done her little service in saving her life. She thrust the thought away, for what would become of her grandfather without her?

Helplessly, she knew that it was a fate to which she could not abandon him. There was no escape. She was trapped here as surely as if she was a prisoner.

CHAPTER
TWO

By dawn the first hint of the day's heat was already evident as a faint breeze stirred the curtains but gave no relief. Verity pressed a hand to her head to ease its aching. A storm would help to break the tension that seemed to hang everywhere, but the air was stifling and heavy.

She had slept badly, haunted by nightmares, and in the mirror now she saw an image barely recognisable as her own, her eyes a vivid green against the flush of her cheeks. Had there ever been a ship, or a man, or were both part of the dream from which she had wakened, trembling at the memory of a stranger's lips upon hers? Could any mere dream have been so real, left her emotions in such turmoil that her heart thudded even now? Turning away she began to brush her hair vigorously, as if the action could banish her thoughts, but they returned, traitorously, and as she became aware of Margaret watching her anxiously, she knew that there was little she could ever conceal from her old nurse. There was a depth of understanding between herself and the woman who had cared for her in place of the mother she had lost, and yet she had discovered in herself a reluctance to share the details of what had happened, even with Margaret.

A hand came to rest on her brow and Verity shrugged it away, frowning. Any fever she may have owed nothing to a chill and she moved away from the discerning grey eyes.

'It's the weather,' she sighed. 'I wish we could have a storm to clear the air.'

Margaret regarded her solemnly. 'There'll be storm enough when your aunt catches you.'

It was a fact Verity had been avoiding. Her hair hung loose about her shoulders in thick, auburn waves, small tendrils clinging to her cheeks. Resentfully she thrust the long tresses into the confines of a white linen cap, securing the ribbons beneath her chin. She hated wearing it, but on the very first day of her arrival at Kingswood her aunt's gaze had flickered sharply over the richness of it and her small mouth had pursed bitterly.

'A woman's hair should not be flaunted. Cover it, girl, or I shall order it to be cropped.'

Verity had complied, suppressing the tears which had welled up. For her grandfather's sake she obeyed, just as she had remained silent when her pretty gowns were taken away and replaced by the drab, black attire approved by her aunt. Her grandfather was too ill for her to wish him to be obliged to take her part against Aunt Harriet's growing authority in his house. It was soon after Aunt Harriet's arrival, in fact, that he had suffered the seizure which had confined him to his room and, from that moment on, Verity had cared for nothing except that he should live and not leave her entirely alone.

She stared with distaste at the black gown, its plainness relieved only by its white collar and cuffs. Beneath it her body bloomed, like a flower doomed never to see the sun, she thought, resentfully. She hated the gown with an intensity matched only by her hatred of her aunt's Puritanical belief that even the simplest of pleasures must be sinful. If womanhood was a sin, then it was a sin she could not avoid and she was glad of it.

Her chin rose defiantly as she fled from the room and tiptoed, breathlessly, along the passages towards the kitchen door. Opening it quietly she stepped out into the deserted yard and, holding up her skirts, ran across the cobbles to a corner which was shielded from the house. Having gained it she leaned thankfully against a wall and stretched her arms upwards as if to grasp at freedom. It was good to breathe in fresh air, untainted by the atmosphere of the house, where the heady perfume of the last of the summer roses lingered. Away from the cove there was no sign of mist. Up here the air was still with the threat of thunder and in the distance the sea had that strange, pewter grey which heralds a storm.

It was still very early. The servants were only just beginning to stir. She could hear the clanking of a pail in the stables and walked towards the sound. The door was half open and she stood watching, her nostrils filling with the scent of warm hay and horses.

A figure turned at her approach.

'Morning, Mistress Verity.'

'Good morning, Tom.' She smiled at the tall, sweating figure of the groom. Thomas Rudd had been with her grandfather for many years. It was he had put her father into the saddle for the first time and then, later, encouraged her own attempts to ride.

'You're about early,' he said, and she pulled a face.

'I couldn't sleep. Anyway, it's the nicest time of day, when everything is quiet.'

The lines in his leathery, tanned face deepened. He knew of the dislike between herself and her aunt, and her reasons for wanting to escape.

'Aye. I like it too.' He stared towards the sea, wiping his brow. 'It's hard to believe there's a war, sometimes.'

'Some day it will be over,' she said, fiercely. 'We shall have a King again.'

'Some day, God willing,' he said, softly, 'but you'd best not let Mistress Ashbourne catch you talking so.'

He was right. She pushed an escaping curl beneath her cap. It was unwise for anyone to speak of the King in these times, yet her heart rebelled at such madness, for madness it was when a kingdom was torn apart and brother even fought brother.

He bent to his task of forking fresh hay and she wandered out into the yard again. She paused at the fish-pond to watch the shadowy carp lying in the green depths, until her fingers rippled the water, disturbing their peaceful existence.

From the yard she could stare across the park towards the woods. Sometimes there were deer to be seen grazing. In spring she would pick bluebells and primroses. She knew every path, but now they were strewn with mouldering leaves and it seemed an eternity until spring would come again.

The dairy was cool and she entered its shade with a sigh of relief. One of her daily tasks was to collect a pitcher of milk and take it to the kitchens. There were cheeses on the shelves and fresh butter. She came often to watch it being made and shaped on the marble slabs which were always ice-cold to the touch, no matter what the time of year. Today she lingered. Sooner or later her aunt or Prudence were bound to discover her, but for the moment at least she was safe.

Defiantly she dragged the restricting cap from her head, letting her hair tumble in golden waves about her shoulders. She smiled as, from the darkest corner of the dairy, a cat emerged and she bent to fondle his ears as he brushed against her gown, voicing his approval of her presence there.

'Poor Humpkin, so this is your favourite place too.' He slid away to roll on the cool flagstones at her feet, eyeing her speculatively and rising to brush at her feet again as she poured milk from a large pail into a pitcher.

She was singing softly to herself, so absorbed in her task that she was unprepared for the voice coming from behind her and spun round, sending the pitcher crashing to the floor where its contents spilled and spread.

'So this is where you are, you sly creature. Did you think you could hide for ever?' Prudence's blue eyes narrowed maliciously. 'Mama wants to see you. You've been neglecting your work again and she is angry.'

Verity faced her cousin, thinking yet again that, at seventeen, Prudence might be pretty were it not for the perpetual scowl which disfigured her features.

Prudence, you startled me. Why must you creep like that?'

The girl leaned against the doorway, her head tilted. 'I didn't creep. You were singing or you would have heard me. You know what mama says about singing.' Her gaze rose, spitefully, 'And where is your cap? Why aren't you wearing it?'

Verity sighed. Humpkin was standing on the offending item, lapping greedily at the fresh cream. He growled when she bent to retrieve it from beneath his wet paws.

'Why are you never to be found when you are needed?' Prudence demanded, haughtily. 'Where do you go?'

For some reason she couldn't explain, Verity felt a sudden wariness sweep over her. She felt reluctant to mention the cove and, even more, the stranger. She was glad of the dim light as her colour rose at the memory of that encounter. Never before had her senses been stirred by a man. She had never imagined that a mere kiss could leave her weak and trembling with mingled fear and anticipation of what it might lead to, a desire to discover strange new emotions. She looked at Prudence, saw the sullenly pursed lips. At the time she hadn't taken seriously the stranger's warning not to speak of his presence in the cove, but now she held back. 'I just walk and lose track of the time.'

'You lazy, good-for-nothing creature, always dreaming instead of tending to your tasks.' Prudence's blue eyes flashed. 'Well, you'll be sorry.' A smile flickered about her mouth, even more disturbing than that previous anger. 'You think yourself far too high and mighty. It would serve you right if mama were to turn you out and leave you and that old man to your own devices.'

Verity flinched but her chin rose. 'Turn *me* out? I think you forget that this is grandfather's house and that but for his charity you and your mother would be homeless now.'

It was worth saying it to hear Prudence's gasp of

surprise, but she had long since learned that in such battles she could only be the loser.

Her cousin's face was brilliant with colour. 'Why you . . . insolent creature.' She advanced into the dairy, her gaze flicking spitefully over the escaped auburn hair. 'I'll make you sorry. You'll regret having made an enemy of me when you have nothing. See what will become of you then. So much for your father and his fine ways. A pity he didn't share the fate traitors deserve along with your precious King.'

In a haze of blind fury Verity's hand rose and even before she herself was aware of her intent, struck a resounding blow.

'My father was no traitor. It was yours who abandoned the King and in doing so nearly killed our grandfather with grief. It is you who should be sorry.'

Prudence shrieked with fury, her eyes brilliant with pain as she clutched at her cheek. Her foot made sharp contact with the cat's tail. Humpkin reared, spitting furiously. Claws flashed and sank into Prudence's flesh, provoking a further howl of rage. She stared furiously at the cat, the colour draining from her face.

'Witches have familiars. That cat must be yours. You commanded him to attack me.'

Verity stared, incredulous, laughter bubbling from her lips as she bent to pick up the cat. His fur stood on end and she whispered, soothingly, her eyes bright with mirth as she held him out to Prudence. 'How can you say such foolish things. As if this poor creature could harm you. Look, he's quite docile.'

Prudence backed away, her pale face distorted

with fury. 'Don't come any closer. I shall tell mama and you'll be sorry.'

'Prudence,' Verity flung out a hand, but it was too late, her cousin had fled, sobbing, towards the house. Gently she held the cat to her cheek. 'Poor Humpkin, we have a lot in common. No one really wants either of us.' Setting him down she returned desolately to the house to face Aunt Harriet's inevitable wrath.

She had flung herself face down on the bed until the first edge of pain began to subside at last. It was as if her aunt had been possessed. The birch had risen again and again until she had cried out and even Prudence had finally protested, dragging her mother away. They had left her then. After a while she had managed to sit up and finally to stand and make her way to her room, wincing as the bruises began to throb. She must have slept, for when she opened her eyes again the warm patch of sun had moved and she was cold. Slowly she put her feet to the floor and got up, just as the door opened and her old nurse came into the room. The old woman's eyes lifted shrewdly to the girl's face and her eyes narrowed. She missed nothing, but knew by the obstinate set of the girl's mouth that probing would bring no answers, not that she had any need of them. Quietly she went to the pitcher which stood on a small table and moistened a cloth with a little water. Ignoring Verity's protests she pressed it to the already darkening bruises and felt the girl flinch.

'Should you be here?' Verity asked.

Meg muttered something beneath her breath,

contempt kindling in her old eyes as her glance flicked to the door. 'I'll answer to that creature the day she's mistress of this house and not before.' She shuffled across the room and took a jar from a casket, applying a lotion to the bruises. Meg knew all about cures and simples. 'Some day I'll tell you all I know about mixing potions,' she said. 'I was taught by my mother and yours would have taught you had she lived, God rest her poor soul. Aye, and perhaps she's better where she is, spared the sight of what England is come to.'

Past sixty, Meg's memory encompassed three reigns. She had recollections of the days when good Queen Bess had sat upon the throne. The good days when a mere slip of a woman had ruled, but the likes of Harry Tudor's lass would never be seen again, more was the pity. The old woman bent to kindle sparks from the dying fire and the flames cast a sallow glow over her leathery features. She cackled softly under her breath.

A momentary flicker of fear passed through Verity. Her mother had spoken once of Meg bearing the mark of a witch and though she herself had laughed at such talk, she had warned that there were those who didn't. 'Meg has the power to brew herbs and heal ills,' she had said. 'People are afraid of what they don't understand and when troubles come they like to lay the cause of it at someone's door, therefore they credit her with the power to cause evil too. Their minds are simple and all the more dangerous because of it.'

Verity had never believed in the talk of witchcraft, but she was filled with a sense of apprehension now, as she smoothed back her long hair from the bruise.

'Don't court trouble for my sake,' she said, sharply.

The old woman frowned. Her eyes dwelt on the girl's slender body, the waist so tiny that a man could span it easily with his hands, and the curves of her breasts, thrusting beneath the plain gown. The child had become a woman, as yet unaware of her own sensuousness. It was there, in the fullness of her mouth and the wide green eyes staring at her defiantly now.

'There are some who don't need to court trouble, it comes looking for them,' she muttered. 'I see trouble ahead for you, and danger.'

Her voice trailed away as if some vision which she alone could see had faded.

Verity had stood stock still. Now she moved, as if coming out of a trance, her face white as she moved towards the door. 'I've no time for your foolishness. I must go to my grandfather.' She left Meg muttering under her breath, but though she tried to dismiss the words they stayed with her and she was still frowning as she entered her grandfather's room.

He sat slumbering before the fire and she stood for a moment, watching him. Each time she did so she was filled with compassion, for in spite of his sixty years, John Ashbourne was still a handsome man. His manservant, Jacob Reymes, rose at her entrance. Smiling, she signalled to him not to wake her grandfather, and crossed to the fire. In the pale glow of the flames his once dark hair and neatly trimmed beard shone white. Such was the brutality of this war that it aged men before their time. It had left its imprint on all of them, but on him more than most. He had faced the death of his eldest son, her own father, and the betrayal of his youngest who had chosen to abandon the beliefs in which he had been raised. But it was the execution of the King which had wreaked the greatest havoc, turning him into the frail thing he had become, as if it marked the futility of the loss of his sons, as if it had all been for naught.

He stirred as if becoming aware of her presence and she moved closer, resting a hand reassuringly on his shoulder. His sight was failing as well now, mocking the liveliness which was still in his eyes.

She bent to light a taper from the fire and he frowned, following the sound of her movements as she crossed the floor.

'Is it night already, child?'

'Not yet, grandfather, but it grows dark early.' She stood at the window, staring out at the wedge of shadow marking the lawns below. A sudden gust of wind gathered up mounds of dead leaves, dancing with them for a moment before casting them down against a wall. Another year drawing to a close and still the turmoil raged between Parliament and King. She sighed, gazing up at the sky. Surely, some day, sanity must return, this war which divided families must end. 'I think we shall have a storm. I'll light the candles and close the shutters.' She moved a pewter sconce closer to his arm, but not so close that he might accidentally dislodge it. Her hand shielded the flame and she saw his nostrils quiver at the smell of the wax. She guided his hand to the warmth of the flame so that he knew where it stood and he nodded.

'Leave the shutters a while yet. I like to feel the air. Come and sit here beside me, child.'

She went gladly. Despite the difference in their

years there was a bond between them which had deepened because of their need of each other. She sighed unconsciously and the old man, ever alert for sounds, heard it.

'Something troubles you, child.' He wished he could see more of her features than mere shadows. 'What is it? Is there news?'

'No, Grandfather, no news.' She reassured him quickly and saw his mouth tighten as hope died in him.

He frowned. 'It is more than a month since the King's army fled Worcester. There should be some word by now.'

She glanced, helplessly, towards his manservant, Jacob Reymes, who shook his head. It became less easy for both of them to find words of comfort now.

'If Charles Stuart had been taken we would have heard. Cromwell would have made much of it.'

His hand raked through his beard as he rose, rejecting the servant's help. 'How can it all have gone so wrong in so short a space? Only a few months ago Scotland proclaimed him King and he had an army of twenty-thousand men. He had but to march to London.'

Reymes's thin figure bent to draw back the covers on the bed. 'Cromwell had all the advantages, and the Scots were too busy dithering between Crown, conscience and Covenant. Time was of the essence.'

'If only Leslie had not turned traitor . . .'

'Alas, we know that that was not the only cause of his failure, Sir John.' Reymes spoke softly, almost warily, 'There was disloyalty even amongst those who stood closest to the King. Buckingham . . .'

'Buckingham.' Her grandfather spat the word. 'His ambition is as great as that of his father before him.' He shook his head. 'It has been an ill year.'

Verity faced him, distress darkening her lovely eyes. 'It is done, Grandfather.' She poured a glass of wine, clasping his hands about it. It pained her to see him so thin, as if he had lost all heart to live.

'I am old.' His hand reached for hers. 'I don't fear for myself, but what is to become of you?'

A chill of fear crept over her, yet she managed to smile. 'You have no cause to fear for me, Grandfather.'

'Times are hard and will grow harder for royalists, girl.'

She knelt before him. 'We must believe that one day the King will come into his own again,' she said. 'While he still lives there is hope.'

'But for how long will he live, with Parliament hunting him like a dog in his own land?' He stared at the fire as if seeing images conjured there. 'France, if only he could get to France. There is no shame in running to fight again.'

She left him rather than let him sense her own desperation, and went to stand at the window. Spots of rain slid down the small panes and she traced their pattern with her finger. 'France seems so far away.'

'But they would shelter him. The Queen Mother, Henrietta Maria, is French-born.'

'If she would only forget her private ambitions,' Reymes said. 'She would see him wed to a Papist and the English will never tolerate it. Are they likely to forget that it was her Catholic influence upon the late King which brought us to this bloody war?'

Verity stared at the two, troubled. 'The new King is still very young. Would he have the strength to fight off her persuasions and those of her French kin?'

'He may be young, but he has a rare strength of character, otherwise he would not have survived thus far,' Sir John reminded her. 'And surely it is better to go to France than die here. It needs but one ship and a loyal crew.'

Suddenly her heart was pounding in her breast as she half turned. A ship. Was it possible? Hope leapt only to be banished. Who would dare it? 'Cromwell knows he cannot afford to let him live. All over England he is hunted and there are so many who would betray him.'

'There are also those who remain loyal.' His voice rasped. 'It needs but one man . . .'

'One man against the might of Cromwell's army, Grandfather.'

'It would need courage and more. The will to kill or be killed. A ruthlessness few men possess.'

Her hand stirred the curtains. 'Someone without pity,' she murmured, 'but where is such a man?'

CHAPTER
THREE

A VOICE penetrated the depths of unconsciousness and she dragged herself reluctantly from the mists of sleep.

'Wake up, quickly.'

Startled, she struggled up from a mound of covers to find Meg standing over her, shaking her roughly. She was about to protest when something in the woman's expression filled her with alarm. Trying desperately to push back the edges of exhaustion she watched as Meg crossed as quickly as her ample body would allow to the window, half pulling back the curtain. With a shock Verity realised that it was not yet fully daylight. She shivered. The fire had long since died in the hearth and a thin glazing of frost covered the window. With her arms huddled about her she sat up, stifling a yawn. 'For pity's sake, what is it? It's scarcely dawn.'

The old woman turned quickly, a finger pressed to her lips as she nodded in the direction of the courtyard below.

'Troopers.'

The very word was sufficient to bring a gasp of horror to the girl's lips. Verity rose quickly, dragging a blanket from the bed and swathing it about her as she padded across the floor to stare at the column of riders milling about the courtyard. The blood ran chill in her veins as she watched their progress to the steps which led up to the house. She was trembling. Roundheads. A dozen men and a wagon came to a halt. She saw one tall figure half turn in his saddle to bark out a command before he dismounted, dragging the helmet from his head. Even at such a distance she could see that he wore his hair cropped short, though not as short as some of Cromwell's army wore it for it still curled about his neck.

She was incapable of movement as she stared at the man who represented the cause of all their present grief. A fierce hatred burned within her and her hands tightened until the nails bit into her palms. If only she had a gun, it would be so easy to kill him. One small act of revenge for all that Cromwell had taken from her, yet she must stand here, helpless, the anger seething in her until it seemed ready to consume her. Then, as if he had become aware of her scrutiny, almost as if the strength of her feelings had somehow conveyed themselves to him, he turned swiftly, and in the next instant a pair of dark, merciless eyes stared into hers.

The blood drained from her face. She sagged weakly against the curtain, stifling a sob of disbelief. In the one moment hatred and desire burned into the very depths of her soul. The ground tilted crazily beneath her. Even in the grey dawn light there could be no mistake. She was staring into the face of her enemy, a man whose cause she despised, yet only hours since that sensuous mouth had claimed hers, his arms had held her, drawing such a strength of emotions from her that she could still tremble at the memory of it. For an instant surprise blazed into the eyes which stared up at her, then she drew back.

Shock took her somehow back to the bed where she sat, trying to fight off the faintness which had enveloped her. It couldn't be. It wasn't possible. In one blinding flash she realised now why he had been at such pains to keep his presence in the cove secret. Sickness tightened her throat. He was a spy. His duty was to trap fleeing royalists and by her silence she had unwittingly aided him. She sat frozen, feeling the tears slide over her cheeks. He had used her. A feeling of hatred swept through her as she rose unsteadily to her feet. Somehow he must be stopped, yet how? Her grandfather was powerless to help her. Her aunt and cousin certainly wouldn't. Never in her life before had she felt so helpless, so utterly alone. She was trembling with emotion and terror. Her enemy was completely unscrupulous and she was entirely within his power.

Dressing quickly she went downstairs to find the entire household had been roused and was in uproar. The outer door had been flung open and from it she could see troopers milling about the courtyard, watering their horses. The groom, Thomas Rudd, was protesting volubly as the stables were commandeered.

In the midst of the noise Harriet Ashbourne appeared, still in her night attire, a robe thrown about her shoulders, a cap set upon her greying curls.

'In the name of heaven, what is happening?'

'It seems we have uninvited guests, Aunt,' Verity said, softly. Then, even as she spoke, a figure strode up the steps, thrusting the door wide with one gloved hand to stand frowning at the two startled women.

Verity froze, her lips parted as for what seemed an eternity she waited for his recognition. Incredibly, it failed to come. Instead the dark eyes narrowed, sweeping her from head to toe with a cold arrogance which drove the colour from her cheeks, before he strode into the hall, his booted feet echoing on the polished floor.

'Who is master here?' Without waiting for a reply he moved to the window and stared down at the movements of his troop below. He drew off his gloves and thrust back his cloak, revealing the blue coat of the parliamentarian regiment worn beneath breast and back plates and the metal gorget.

The look of satisfaction which settled on her aunt's face sickened Verity.

'My late husband's father, Sir John Ashbourne, is the owner.'

His gaze veered swiftly over their dress as his expression darkened. 'The Ashbournes are royalist.'

Harriet Ashbourne drew herself up haughtily. 'Not all, Captain. My daughter and I were obliged to seek the charity of a roof over our heads, but that does not mean we have abandoned our beliefs. You are most welcome here.'

A flicker of curiosity touched his gaze as he moved from the window. 'This is your daughter?'

Verity held her breath as he came closer, frowning. She longed to cry out, to denounce him, but the words stuck in her throat. Denounce him as what? The man who had made so easy a conquest of her emotions in a moment when she had needed comfort, a man who had seduced her with his charm, taken advantage of her naivete? Her cheeks burned, then from somewhere behind them a ripple of quiet laughter intruded.

Prudence was standing on the stairs. 'You do me an injustice, Captain.' Her voice rose haughtily, 'My cousin is a royalist to the depths of her black little soul, but not I.' She advanced slowly, a smile playing about her lips as she crossed the floor and made a slight curtsey before the man whose admiration was evident.

With a sense of shock, Verity realised that Prudence was flaunting herself deliberately. She was wearing only a thin shift above her night gown and her hair, as yet free of the linen cap, hung about her shoulders in a riot of blonde curls. The blue eyes flashed with contempt in her own direction and she shrank before the malice in them. 'Yes, indeed you are welcome, Captain, Captain . . . ?'

'Richard Kingston, Mistress Ashbourne.' He tore his gaze with reluctance from her to the older woman. 'I regret, for your sakes, Ma'am, that it will be necessary for me to billet my men here.'

Before she had even time to consider her words, Verity said scathingly, 'You mean that you will live as the rest of your kind, like leeches off others.' She recoiled instantly, expecting anger. Instead he regarded her coolly, as if she were a mere child, yet there was a note of warning in his voice which made her tremble.

'Traitors have no rights, Mistress, you would do well to remember that. It is in the power of the Lord Protector to confiscate all property and possessions of known royalists.' His mouth compressed. 'I will see Sir John Ashbourne.'

Her head rose sharply. 'My grandfather is a sick man. He can do you no harm. He has suffered enough. Can you not leave him in peace?'

'Be silent, girl.' Her aunt's voice rapped harshly. 'Thus far you have been too lucky.'

Verity moistened her dry lips. Ignoring her aunt she appealed directly to the man who stared with cold impassiveness down at her.

'The shock will kill him. Isn't it enough that you are here? Why can you not go about your devilish business and leave him in peace.' She stared hard into his face, but to her dismay saw no hint of remorse. Instead the dark eyes merely narrowed and she shuddered.

'Understand me clearly, Mistress,' he said in a dangerously low tone. 'I have a job to do and nothing and no one will be permitted to stand in my way.' Flicking a glove against his palm he strode past her, pushing open doors and surveying her grandfather's library. Her heart fell as he nodded. 'This will suit my purpose admirably.' He flung down the gloves and a leather despatch bag.

'May we know the purpose of your presence in these parts, Captain?' Harriet Ashbourne enquired.

He stared from the window, frowning as he studied the outlying land. His attention flickered impatiently back to the woman. 'We have reason to believe that royalists are escaping to France, using vessels anchorred offshore locally. It is possible the traitor Charles Stuart may be among them.'

'It will be better for England when we are rid of that scourge.'

'Indeed, Madam. Are those woods over there?'

Prudence was beside him. 'Yes, they are.'

His glance softened as he looked down at her. 'And beyond them?'

'A path which leads to the cove.'

He smiled, and to Verity who watched, sickened by the spectacle, it was as if, for a moment, her rescuer stood before her again. 'I shall ride over the area. Perhaps you will accompany me, Mistress Ashbourne, and tell me all I need to know.'

'I shall be pleased to, Captain.'

Anger flared in Verity. 'But surely you are already well versed with such knowledge, Captain Kingston?' She flung out the challenge and was gratified to see the flicker of alarm which sprang suddenly to his eyes as he faced her.

'You are mistaken, Mistress.' Before she realised it he was so close that she could feel the warmth of his breath upon her face and in spite of herself her legs trembled. She was not mistaken. How could she be? Suddenly tears pricked at her eyes at the memory of the tenderness of an embrace and she willed him to confess that, for a moment at least, they had shared love. She saw no response, the eyes were coldly impersonal, cruel. 'I have ridden direct from London at the command of the Lord Protector himself.'

She gasped at the blatant lie, defiance gleaming in her eyes. She opened her mouth to speak, but even as she did so her wrist was caught in a vice-like grip as his fingers closed over it and any words she might have uttered were stifled in a sob of pain.

'You are . . . hurting me.' The more she fought the tighter she was held until she sagged faintly against him. At once she became aware of the warmth and physical strength of him and traitorous colour swept into her cheeks.

'I see your cousin is right. It will be necessary for me to keep you under close watch,' he thrust her away. 'And now, I will see Sir John Ashbourne.'

'Oh . . .' She winced as she rubbed at her bruised wrist. 'I despise you.'

He laughed softly, yet there was no humour in the sound. 'Hatred brings with it a healthy respect, Mistress, and you would be wise to respect me.'

She shuddered, his face a pale blur before her now.

'Be silent, you wicked creature.' Aunt Harriet's mouth was pursed grimly. 'Do what you must, Captain, there will be no hindrance from this house.'

Verity was aware of the smirk which played about her cousin's lips and remembered the conversation she had unwittingly overheard upon her return from the cove. Fear dulled defiance. Were they to lose this house now the shock would kill her grandfather, yet she saw no hint of remorse on Prudence's pretty face.

Richard Kingston strode to the door. 'I have commandeered the stables and sufficient feed for our horses. My men will billet in the stables and barn and this house will be under constant surveillance.'

'You have no reason to fear, Captain,' Harriet Ashbourne began, only to find her words dismissed as his glance flickered over Verity.

'I have my duty and it is not unknown for royalists to hide in what are thought to be safe houses, Madam.' He turned on his heel and mounted the stairs towards her grandfather's room.

Without waiting for her aunt's dismissal, she fled blindly from the room and out to the yard, glad to breathe in the fresh air. She paused for a moment, closing her eyes and feeling the tears trickle down her face. She was vaguely aware of the troopers.

One called out and they all laughed. She gathered up her skirts and ran, despising them all. He was of their kind. How could she have been such a fool?

Gaining the safety of the dairy she entered its cool dimness and leaned weeping against the door. Her mind was in turmoil. Richard Kingston had walked into her life again, this time to threaten its very foundations, and she was entirely powerless against him. She despised all he stood for, yet why then did her heart deny it and play the traitor?

Returning to the house later she made her way quickly to her grandfather's room only to find the door guarded by a sentry. Trying to pass, her way was barred roughly by the trooper who caught at her arm.

'No one enters by orders of the Captain.'

Her heart sank in despair as she drew back. From within the room she could hear the muffled sound of voices, one raised in anger, though the words themselves were indistinct. Her face paled at the thought of Richard Kingston interrogating her grandfather. He would show no mercy.

'I must go to my grandfather, he is sick.'

The man leered insolently, his eyes dwelling on her slender figure with a gleam of excitement. She withdrew her arm sharply and stared helplessly at the door, her fists clenching. The trooper smiled speculatively.

'Try later, mistress, when the Captain has gone. I'd not be so churlish as to refuse a maid leave to see her grandsire were she to oblige me with some little reward for my pains.'

The man grinned and she felt her cheeks grow hot beneath his gaze. Without a word she turned and fled and for once was glad of the duties which kept her occupied, even of the extra tasks her aunt suddenly found for her to perform.

'It will do you good to learn a little humility at last, my fine miss.' The small eyes regarded her haughtily. 'Times are changing. With the Stuart gone England will see a return to Godliness again.'

Verity lowered her eyes, sickened by the fervour in her aunt's eyes. Silently she went about her tasks, hating the need to carry milk and water to the stables where the troopers greeted her with crude jests which made her escape, leaving the pails behind.

By mid-morning the late October sun was sending a heat haze shimmering over the yard and flies skimmed the pond. She was collecting eggs from the hen-house and wearily pushing stray strands of golden hair beneath her cap when she saw the tall figure striding from the house towards her.

Richard Kingston stood before her and she felt the flush creep up into her cheeks as his steely glance was directed down at her. She was aware yet again of the strength in the tall, broad-shouldered figure, of the arrogance which seemed to warn that if she dared to challenge him she would be subdued as easily as any child. She closed her eyes, wishing she could as easily blot out the memory of his lips claiming her own with such passion, and when she opened them again it was almost as if she had caught him off guard, surprising some expression in him, a look of concern . . . She laughed at her own foolishness then. She had been fooled once, but never again.

'What have you done to my grandfather?' she demanded, and as if he sensed the fear beneath her defiance his eyes narrowed, mockingly.

'I found him stubborn, but there was never any doubt that he would tell me what I wished to know.'

She gasped at such ruthlessness. 'Have you no pity?'

He moved closer, his voice dispassionate. 'None at all, Mistress. You would be foolish to imagine otherwise. I have warned you that I have a duty to perform.'

'Duty?' A bitter smile twisted her lips. 'You are a spy.' Incredibly, she saw him flinch and regretted the words as anger flooded into his eyes. She backed away only to come to a halt, imprisoned by the stone wall at her back and his arm which came to rest upon it, brushing against her cheek.

His voice was little more than a whisper yet he left her in no doubt of his anger. 'You are being very foolish, Mistress Ashbourne.' His face was very close to her own. She could feel the warmth of his breath on her cheek and was conscious of the thudding of her heart.

'My grandfather knows nothing which could be of any possible value to you. Is this how brave Cromwell's army fights its war, by torturing old men and women?' She tried to laugh, but the sound rasped hoarsely in her throat.

The arm which imprisoned her was removed. 'It is as well that you know that, if necessary, I will use any means,' he said, softly. 'He is a royalist, that is enough. Old loyalties die hard and I see he has bred them in you.' Before she could prevent it his hand had flicked out and was behind her head, forcing her closer. 'Despite this garb you wear, the heart that beats under it is royalist to the core. Your cousin is right, you are dangerous.'

Her green eyes flashed defiance as she jerked

free. 'I make no secret of it. I despise you and all that you stand for. Were it possible I would kill you with my own hands.'

He laughed, softly, cruelly, then his arms imprisoned her and his lips came down upon hers, brutally silencing her protests. He forced her head back as one hand twisted in her long hair and the other pinned her close to him. She fought and sobbed, yet even as she struggled to break free, desire surged like a wave and she submitted, meeting his passion, craving satisfaction of her own. He moaned and then she was released, so abruptly that she all but fell. For one moment he stared down at her then, cold as steel, he laughed as he straightened up. 'I have given you fair warning, lady. I take what I want and nothing and no one will stand in my way.'

Before she could speak he had turned and was striding away, leaving her to stare after him, her emotions stripped naked, her mouth bruised by that kiss.

Moments later she saw him ride away from the house with Prudence beside him. Her cousin's face was flushed prettily and she wore her best gown. Harriet Ashbourne watched their departure, a smile of satisfaction momentarily softening her face as she stood beside her niece.

'They make a fine pair, your cousin and the Captain. I believe he has no wife. Imagine the honour one would have as the wife of a man acknowledged to be close to the Lord Protector.'

Somehow Verity forced herself to speak. 'As you say, Aunt, they make a fine pair.' Grateful that her aunt had failed to notice the flush in her own cheeks she sped away, hurrying towards the house where she carried the basket of eggs to the kitchens before making her way to her grandfather's room.

To her relief there was no sentry posted outside the door and she went in quickly. He was seated by the window which Jacob Reymes had opened at his insistence.

From below the sound of men and horses floated up and as he listened his brows drew together until she moved close, then his frail hand took hers as she spoke.

'I came as quickly as I could. Did he harm you?'

He shook his head, but his eyes were troubled. 'No, child. But there is danger. You must be very careful.'

She looked at him, troubled by the expression in his eyes.

'Why? What would the Captain want with me? I can do him no harm. Would to God I could.'

To her surprise he responded angrily. 'That is foolish talk.'

'Then I cannot help it, Grandfather. I hate him and all he stands for.' She rose and left him, crossing to the window where she stood, half concealed by the curtains. She clasped her arms about her. In spite of the heat of the fire she felt as if the warmth had suddenly drained from her body. 'I am afraid, Grandfather. What hope is there for the King when he is hunted by such men? What chance have we against him and his kind? Dear God, how I hate him.'

His head rose, sharply. 'There are times when it is wiser to be silent, child. They will not harm us as long as we do as we are told. You must obey the Captain.'

She turned, gasping with disbelief at the words. 'I don't understand. How can you say such things when all my life you have taught me that my loyalty must be to the King above all things, that he rules by Divine Right. My father died fighting for his own belief in that right and now you tell me I must obey this . . . this traitor?' Her voice broke with humiliation.

His hand caught sharply at hers as she moved to kneel before him. 'I don't ask it of you, child, I demand it.'

Her face went whiter yet. 'No, Grandfather, I cannot do it.'

'I am too old and you haven't the strength to fight him alone. There are times when pride must seem to be humbled. Trust me.'

She shook her head, horrified to hear him speak so. Tears hung unshed on her lashes. 'I cannot, will not, believe that you mean this. I will die rather than see such a man destroy all I believe in.'

His voice rose with an anger she had never in her life heard before.

'Child, you will obey me.'

Stricken she drew back, biting at her lip. 'You don't know what you are saying, what you ask of me.'

His expression softened. 'I am well aware of it, but my fear is only for you.'

'And mine for you, but . . .'

'Then for all our sakes, I beg you, do not cross this man.'

Her hand withdrew from his and she frowned, bewildered by what seemed his betrayal. 'What did he say to you?' she asked, quietly. 'What means did he use to threaten you that you can speak so to me?

You were never afraid before.'

The near-sightless eyes searched her face and she was desolated to see him looking so drawn and exhausted. 'Trust me,' he said.

'I always have and always will.'

'Then do nothing.'

Desperately she moved away. 'How can I do as you ask?' For the first time in her life all her fears and doubts seemed to come together to challenge him. 'It is not only his presence in this house but the timing of it . . .' Her voice faded. 'There are things you too don't understand.' She clasped her hands together. 'I have reason to believe that Captain Richard Kingston may be even more dangerous than we imagine.'

'What do you mean?'

She hesitated, even now reluctant to speak. 'I . . . I said nothing to you because I . . . I was unsure even in my own mind, but now it is different. Grandfather, something is very wrong. This man comes here as a stranger. He claims to have come from London, yet I know that he is lying.' For a moment there was silence. She saw the expression pass quickly between her grandfather and Jacob Reymes and his voice, when he spoke, was grim.

'You are mistaken.'

She shook her head. 'No, Grandfather, I am not mistaken. I have seen him before. Down in the cove.' Colour tinged her cheeks. How could she be mistaken? 'I was walking down on the beach. I thought I saw a ship, then it vanished from sight and I put it down to my imagination. But soon after, this . . . this man who calls himself Richard Kingston, came ashore . . .' She broke off in confusion as her grandfather struggled to raise himself in his chair.

Never before had she seen such anger in his face.

'For pity's sake, child, say no more. Never repeat those words beyond these four walls or more lives than you imagine may be at stake. You were mistaken.'

His hand closed over her arm with such intensity that she winced.

'No, Grandfather.'

'I have never before demanded your word or your obedience. I do so now.'

Protests rose only to be crushed as she saw the expression in his eyes.

'But what if it is the King himself they seek?' she whispered. 'You cannot mean to stand by and let it happen? No, Grandfather, I despise this man and all he stands for. Had I the means I would kill him . . .'

His voice no longer appealed, it was angry. 'Am I to be denied your trust now, after all these years?'

Her voice seemed to be stuck in her throat as she rose quickly to her feet. Tears blinded her. What was the power the stranger seemed to hold over all their lives? She swallowed hard.

'I will try to do as you ask, but I cannot give you my word.' Turning she fled before he could speak again.

CHAPTER
FOUR

VERITY shivered as she went about her task in the great storage barn. She was collecting fruit and herbs for the kitchens. Normally the smell of the apples, plums and pears picked from their own orchards, the bunches of sage and rosemary, the lavender to be scattered amongst clothes and linen in the great oaken chests, was something she loved. Today the scents were cloying and she paused, brushing a hand against her brow. Her head ached. She had slept badly and the shadows beneath her eyes were evidence of it. Darkness had brought not the oblivion she craved, but wakefulness filled with disturbing memories of Richard Kingston's dark eyes staring into her own, the dark hair curling against his neck. Then had come the nightmares from which she had woken, sobbing fretfully. Finally she had got out of bed and dressed, feeling drained and dispirited, but not even daylight offered any real release. It was easy to keep her hands occupied, less easy to command her brain when everywhere she turned there was evidence of the presence of her enemy.

A sudden sound broke her reverie and with a start she went to the door of the barn to stand in the shadows. The courtyard was suddenly full of men and horses milling noisily about. Their breath fanned white into the chill morning air, pale sunlight gleamed on breastplates and helmets. Then her eyes were drawn to one tall figure already in the saddle and suddenly her heart was racing. Richard Kingston moved amongst his men issuing orders and even from where she stood she could see the respect he commanded.

The troopers had formed into columns and were moving towards her. Pressed against the doorway she was aware of the man at their head, his features harsh in the shadows of his helmet. She was incapable of movement. The clattering hooves came closer. Her gaze was fixed upon a pair of leather boots, then the hem of a cloak. She would not look at him. She was trembling so much that her teeth chattered. Then, as if by some compulsion, her gaze rose. His features might have been hewn from stone as he rode past. It was as if he had not even seen her, yet oddly there was no comfort in the thought.

She was breathless when she entered the kitchen moments later and set the baskets on the table. Harriet Ashbourne was busy supervising the salting of the last of the summer vegetables. She looked up impatiently.

'Where have you been, girl? I've been waiting for those things.'

Keeping her eyes lowered, hoping her aunt would not see the sudden colour in her cheeks, she tried to keep the note of curiosity from her voice. 'I'm sorry, Aunt. The yard was full of troopers. Has something happened? Are they leaving?'

Her aunt's gaze sought a large stone jar. 'Happened?' She frowned. 'Get on with your work, girl. I want the stones removed from those plums. What makes you think anything should have happened?'

'The soldiers are leaving.'

Her aunt laughed sharply. 'I'm sure you'd like that. Well, they will be back. Things won't be changed that easily, my girl.'

Verity hid her face quickly. Her hands were trembling as she slit open the juice-filled fruit. Something must have happened to cause the troop to ride out. She tried to speak calmly. 'Is there any news?'

'Not of the sort you would wish to hear, I'll be bound. There has been talk of royalists fleeing from Worcester and heading this way towards the coast. Hoping to find a ship to take them to France, no doubt. Well, they'll not get far.'

Her aunt moved away to supervise the stacking of the stone jars upon the shelves and Verity went about her task wordlessly, her brain in turmoil. Royalists, heading this way? Terror gripped her. But they would be riding straight into danger, unaware of the troopers' presence. Her knuckles clenched round the knife she held and her lips tightened. Was that what the Captain had planned, a trap into which they would stumble blindly? The blade flashed as she plunged it deep into the fruit, wishing it was his black heart, then it clattered to the floor as her fingers jerked from it. Such thoughts were completely alien to her. Never before had she wished any man dead as she now wished Richard Kingston.

She became aware of Prudence watching her, a triumphant smile on her face. She picked idly at the fruit and bit into a plum, licking the juice from her fingers.

'So, your brave royalist friends are on the run.' She laughed at the sudden whiteness of her cousin's face. 'Oh, it will do you no good to hope. They stand no chance. Richard will have every road and every bridge guarded by now.'

Verity pressed her hands against the table in order to still their trembling. The ground seemed to be moving beneath her feet, yet somehow she forced herself to look up, to meet her cousin's gaze.

' "Richard", cousin? Surely my aunt does not approve of such familiarity?'

Prudence laughed. 'How else should I speak of the man I mean to marry?'

Verity's mouth was suddenly dry. 'Marry? How can that be? You have scarcely known him more than a few hours. Has he asked you?'

Prudence's blue eyes flashed. 'What does it matter? He will. We talked of mama and I going to London. Richard has influence.' Her chin rose, haughtily. 'He has the friendship of the Lord Protector himself.'

'I don't doubt it,' Verity was sickened.

'You are jealous.'

'Jealous?' Her fists clenched until the knuckles shone white. 'I despise Richard Kingston and all he stands for.'

'Then I pity you, cousin, for there will be no place for royalists in England once your precious King is dead.'

Prudence flounced away and the morning dragged as Verity was kept fully occupied by her aunt's demands. It was noon before she was able to get away and then she slipped out to the garden, glad to be alone at last.

Here where no one could see she took off her cap and let her hair fall loose in heavy, golden waves. She sat beside the pool, watching fish dart between the dark green lilies, and unbuttoned the collar of her gown, turning her face up to the sun's warmth. Aunt Harriet would have called such abandonment wicked, but for once she didn't care. It was good to be free.

After a while she rose and walked between the neatly clipped hedges, her thoughts in confusion. Never in her life had she questioned or disobeyed her grandfather, but what he asked of her now was a burden too great to bear. How could he forget so easily that it might have been her own father fleeing for his life? Tears pricked at her eyes at the injustice of it. Something far greater than their own lives was at stake. England's only hope for the future lay in Charles Stuart's escape and a ruthless stranger was a threat to that hope and those of all true royalists. How could she be silent and do nothing? No matter what the cost Richard Kingston had to be stopped.

She was walking quickly as if to escape her thoughts, yet she became aware yet again of her own helplessness. What of the ship in the cove? She was convinced it had not been merely a figment of her own imaginings and it would explain only too well the Captain's presence there and his desire for secrecy. Had she stumbled unwittingly into his trap instead, and, in so doing, ruined his plan to discover the ship and capture any fugitives who made towards it?

She leaned against a tree, breathing hard as much from the effort of her walk as from the emotions hammering within her breast. A sense of indescribable desolation swept over her. In any other time but this she might have loved such a man. But then, would he return that love? She closed her eyes, afraid to acknowledge the truth that she was fully aware of Richard Kingston's desire, but desire was not love.

It was the sound of twigs snapping sharply which brought her up with a start to the feeling that she was not alone. She listened, then laughed the thought aside. She had begun to jump at shadows since the troopers' arrival at Kingswood. She moved on, stirring the dead leaves underfoot. Then it came again, this time closer. She spun round, her eyes wide, her heart thudding wildly. There *was* someone.

She backed away. 'Who is it? Who is there?' Her glance darted at the thickness of the overhanging trees and then towards the direction of the house. She had come further than she thought and even if she called for help no one would hear. She began to move, slowly. Why should anyone want to follow her? Holding up the hem of her skirts she started to walk. Branches moved, wind-dried leaves crackled as a foot pressed them into the path behind her. A sob caught in her throat as she began to run. A briar tore at her hand, but she was oblivious to the pain as it ripped into her flesh. There was no longer any doubt, as her own steps quickened so too did those others. Not daring to turn she ran, hearing him close behind—his breath, the grating of his boot as he stepped on a fallen branch.

Sobbing with terror now, she saw the house ahead. Pain twisted like a knife between her ribs and still her pursuer came closer. She had almost reached the stables only to find, to her horror, that the courtyard was deserted. Her fingers clawed at the wooden door then she screamed as she heard muffled laughter and a cloak came down, stifling her cries, trapping her in a terrifying world of dark-

ness from which there was no escape, no matter
how desperately she fought.

Her fingers tore at the heavy fabric. She was
suffocating. She must have air or she would die.
The hands which held her were strong as steel and
suddenly she found herself lifted upwards across
her assailant's shoulders like a sack of grain. Driven
by terror she continued to fight, then, for a hideous
moment, she felt herself hurtling through space.
The stable door crashed to a close as she fell, her fall
miraculously broken by the straw on which she
landed, though her arm jarred sickeningly against
one of the stalls. Pain flooded through her, leaving
her faint and sick, but even as she cried out the
muffling folds which imprisoned her were lifted and
a figure loomed above her.

The scream died in her throat, stilled by terror, as
she stared up at the trooper she had seen on guard
outside her grandfather's room. His face was contorted by a leer of triumph as he looked down at her
with greedy eyes. He stood astride her and slowly
removed his jacket, his gaze never leaving her terrified face. The sight of her fear seemed to inflame
him, yet he was in no hurry. He was savouring his
good fortune, laughing softly as she cowered away
from him.

His intent was obvious. Her mouth opened to
scream with all the power in her lungs, but the
sound never came. His weight crushed down upon
her, the stench of his foul-smelling body filled her
nostrils before his face blotted out the light and his
mouth claimed hers. The kiss was brutal. She
fought, trying desperately to twist her head away,
her fists beating at him, yet it was all in vain. His
strength was such that she was subdued, his one

hand encircling her wrists, leaving her writhing with fear and helplessness.

Her struggles were getting weaker as faintness threatened to overtake her, yet she knew she must not lose consciousness. For one instant his weight shifted and she thought she was free. She was wrong. His hand was beneath her head. She felt his short-cropped hair graze against her face, then his hands were moving over her body, beneath her back, lifting her, moulding her struggling form to his own. Her fingers raked at the naked flesh of his chest, but he was like an animal, oblivious to anything but the satisfaction of his own lust. She wept, her teeth biting into her lip until she could taste the bitterness of blood, and he laughed.

'Don't fight me, my pretty, or I'll have to hurt you. A pretty wench like you don't want to spend the rest of her days in a place like this, her head filled with Puritan cant. James Tulley can teach you a thing or two about the pleasures to be got 'twixt a man and a woman.'

Revulsion swept through her like a physical sickness as his hands moved over her body, tearing clumsily at her bodice until they came to the soft flesh beneath.

Her eyes were blinded by hot tears, her hair in thick, damp strands across her face. His hands were at her back, lifting her, parting her thighs even as he continued to force kisses upon her mouth.

She broke free, sobbing, 'No. No, let me go.'

He moved, laughing softly, but only to fumble at his own clothing, then his breath was hot against her as he pushed the strands of hair from her face and looked down at her triumphantly. Her chin was held and she was forced to look up at him. She felt

her senses beginning to slip away. Dear God, why
did no one hear her cries?

'The Captain shall hear of this . . .'

Brown, uneven teeth showed as he grinned. 'You
think the Captain will care what happens to a
royalist wench?'

Her strength was gone. She was falling, a tide of
blackness sweeping over her. Oblivion would be
merciful now, she welcomed it as she became aware
of his legs roughly parting her own. It was true, why
should the Captain care what happened to her?

From the depths of semi-consciousness she became aware of light flooding in brilliantly as a door
crashed open. She heard voices, one brittle with
rage. Suddenly the weight was falling from her and
she gasped. The scream which had been trapped in
her throat for so long broke forth at last, then arms
held her. She sobbed within their protective
warmth, was aware incredulously of lips gently
brushing against her cheek, murmuring her name.
Dark eyes stared down at her, angry yet full of
concern. She stared back in wonderment. How
could it be? She moved, restlessly, from something
which must be part of the dream, and groaned with
pain.

'Lie still. Dear God, if he has hurt you . . .'

The voice faded. She dimly saw Tulley, his
features contorted with rage. A knife flashed. Somehow she managed to cry out and the Captain turned
swiftly and with a muttered oath closed with the
trooper. In an agony of terror she was forced to
watch, dragging herself to a corner of the stall as the
two figures fought. Tulley lunged, his face ashen.
She saw the blade find its mark, cutting through the
Captain's sleeve, and a faint trickle of blood welled

up, spreading a dark stain on the fabric. Her hand was pressed to her mouth to still a cry. Richard Kingston's mouth was taut, his features angular in the dull shadows of the stable. Suddenly it was for Tulley that she was afraid, yet she felt no pity as she saw the blade fly from his hand before he was lying sprawled in the straw.

The Captain staggered, his hand pressed against the steady flow of blood from his arm. He swayed as he looked up and signalled to one of his men.

'Get him out of here,' he rapped. 'Keep him under arrest until he can be sent to London.' He straightened, brushing a lock of hair from his eyes and he turned to her again. Her heart was behaving oddly. This was the man she hated, yet he had saved her. A multitude of emotions surged through her as she stared up at him, brushing the thick mane of hair from her face.

'You are wounded.' Some sound startled her, but there was nothing but a shadow.

He didn't even glance at his arm. 'It's nothing. A scratch.'

The coldness in his tone shocked her. Somehow she had expected something else yet, incredibly, all the gentleness had gone from him as if it had never been. Her hand rose, shaking, to the bruise on her cheek and she frowned. Perhaps it had after all only been part of the dream. She pulled her skirts down over the nakedness of her legs where the evidence of Tulley's assault was already beginning to show in dark bruises.

'I . . . I owe you my thanks,' she stammered. 'If you hadn't come when you did . . .' The consequences were too awful to contemplate and her cheeks flooded with colour as he stared grimly down at her. Then she remembered something else and her eyes widened. 'Your mission . . . How did you come . . . ?'

His eyes were dark and cruel as they flickered over her and she shrank from the fury in them. 'My mission failed, this time. Which no doubt will please you, Mistress Ashbourne.' He moved closer, staring contemptuously at her torn gown where it revealed the creamy-whiteness of her breasts. Her hair fell in dishevelled waves about her shoulders. His eyes narrowed to glittering slits. 'I fear your efforts were in vain. Perhaps my arrival was a little too timely. A pity. Perhaps I should have let Tulley have his way, then I might have discovered just how far you are prepared to go in order to gain your own ends,' he drawled softly, and the hint of a threat was like a cold shower upon her.

She gasped, unable to believe what she heard. White-faced she cowered before him. 'What are you saying? I don't know what you mean . . .'

He laughed, 'Then let me put it more plainly. I am telling you that your seduction of one of my men failed. Tulley responded a little too well to it, but even had he not, he could have told you nothing of my plans. He would not have betrayed me in any event. My men know too well that I can be entirely ruthless when opposed. Perhaps it is time that you too learned that.'

He moved threateningly closer and even before she was aware of what she did her hand rose and struck him so forcibly that he reeled beneath the blow. His face contorted and, moving with the speed of a cat, he caught her, forcing her down into the straw, his body imprisoning hers with the strength of steel. She fought desperately, yet despite the wound, he held her easily, pinioning her wrists against the straw above her head. She could feel the warm strength of his muscular body straining against her own, then his lips found her mouth, crushing down upon it with a savagery which bruised yet left her drained of strength. The roughness of his coat brushed against her cheek. She hated him with every shred of her being, then, with a sob, felt her body respond like a traitor to him, moving to the rhythm of his desire. Her mouth returned the kiss, savouring it, her lips parting. Miraculously she felt the anger die within him and he groaned as his arms held her to him. She felt the warm nakedness of his chest where his shirt had become unfastened, and in a blinding flash of realisation became aware of what she was doing. She began to struggle to get free. He held her ruthlessly, staring down at her as she lay beneath him, his mouth cruelly mocking.

'Tulley is a simple man, a fool easily enticed by a woman's charms. I mean to show you, Mistress, that if you try them on me, you'll be the one to pay, and dearly, for I'll show you no mercy.'

She jerked helplessly, unable to be free, horror at what she had almost done flooding through her. She could not love this man. *Must* not.

'I . . . hate you,' she wept convulsively. Their eyes met and she saw the pulse beating in his neck. Some expression flickered in his eyes before he released her abruptly.

Dumbly she watched as he rose to his feet and she covered her semi-nakedness, clutching the torn gown to her as she sat up. His gaze mocked her efforts. She might have been completely naked as it raked over her, then, without a word, he strode

away, leaving her to rest her head weakly against a
stall. Tears hung on her cheeks. Her body was
bruised by the violence of those assaults, yet her
mind sought the one comfort to which she must
cling. He had confessed his mission a failure. The
trap he had set had gained him nothing. Was that
why he had vented his anger upon her, as a
revenge? If so, then she feared to see him truly
roused.

After a while she rose to her feet and returned to
the house. To her relief Margaret was busy elsewhere and she was spared the inevitable questions.
She had to get away. Flinging a black cloak about
her, alert for any sound, she crept down the stairs,
fearing at any moment to see someone bar her way,
but no one came.

It was almost dusk as she ran towards the woods.
She had no conscious idea of where she was going,
anywhere, only so long as she didn't have to see
Richard Kingston again just yet. No man had ever
roused such conflicting emotions within her before.
Her steps quickened, as if by running she could
outpace her thoughts, but they stayed to haunt her.
She had abandoned herself for one wild moment to
his kisses and he had triumphed in his power over
her.

The path through the woods was overgrown with
briars that caught at her skirts and tore at her
hands. She was scarcely aware of them, of anything
except the need to be alone. Few people knew this
path, but her own feet found it with ease, her shoes
stirring the mouldering leaves.

The path ended as the wood opened onto the
green of the cliff top. Below the sea sparkled in the
glow of the fading sun and she shivered as the

breeze stirred her hair. Her glance went automatically to the path which led to the cove below, then she sat in the long grass, tucking her billowing skirts about her knees. There was something about the sea which always drew her to it. Its changing moods, wild and restless one minute, calm the next. The tide was nearly at its height now. Within the hour the few remaining rocks where the sea pounded would be submerged and the dark line of shingle hidden.

She stirred restlessly. What devil had made her come here now? The man in whose arms she had stood so willingly that other night bore no resemblance to the ruthless Captain Richard Kingston.

The shadows deepened. The moon cut a silver path across the water and the air had turned cold. She shivered, huddling deeper into the black cloak as she rose reluctantly to her feet. The sea lapped gently below. She paused, listening, then froze as her eye caught the faint flicker of light which cut suddenly out of the darkness.

She drew in her breath. It came again, then again, too regular to be dismissed as mere reflection. Her heart beat wildly. Someone was out there, signalling. A ship. She moved forward as cloud momentarily hid the moon, crouching as her feet sought and found the narrow track which led to the beach below. The light winked into the darkness once more, then, as the moon appeared again, she had to stifle a cry. A great, shadowy shape lay in the water, like some great bird of prey. Her scalp tingled. This time there was no doubt. There was a ship and someone aboard was signalling towards the shore.

CHAPTER
FIVE

It was some moments before the light came again and it was only then that she realised that the vessel was not, as she had imagined, at anchor, but moving slowly from a narrow shoulder of rocks into the cove.

Huddled against the cliff path, she frowned as scudding clouds obscured the moon, but it was only a brief interlude before she made out the dark outline again. Easing her cramped limbs she moved closer, loosening sand and small stones as she did so. The sound drew her up sharply to the awareness that someone else might be close by. Those signals must be intended for someone on the shore. The knowledge made her heart thud uncomfortably, but she had seen no one and it was unlikely that her own silent vigil had been witnessed or some alarm would have been raised. Perhaps the recipient, whoever he was, had been delayed—or was lying in wait.

A sense of exhilaration overcame fear. Whatever she had stumbled upon, it confirmed her belief that she had seen a ship here before. She frowned then, remembering the Captain's interest in this place, and her mouth was suddenly dry. The presence of that ship now could mean only one of two things, that she had come upon him by chance that day, before he had had an opportunity to spring his trap and lure the ship inshore, or that he had been unaware of its presence in the cove. It was only by the merest chance that she had seen it herself, and then so fleetingly that she had almost put it down to her imagination. The thought offered no consolation. If that was the case the cove might still be under observation and the vessel and its crew were in danger, as was anyone who came to keep a rendezvous.

Numb with cold she clambered closer still, feeling the fine spray against her face, dampening her hair. Her feet slipped on the loose, wet stones and with a sharp intake of breath she came to a halt. It was some moments before she heard a sound. The familiarity of it struck a chill into her heart, then she saw the small rowing boat and with a gasp of horror drew back. Someone meant to land, here in this very spot. She cursed herself for having been so foolish as to overlook the possibility and leaving herself vulnerable. It could just as easily be an enemy ship out there. It bore no ensign and she had recklessly put herself close to danger.

As she moved the shingle grated beneath her feet and she froze as the sound seemed to echo in the silence. Too late now to go back even if she could find her way in the darkness. Only a thin edging of beach was left uncovered by the tide and suddenly she prayed for the moon to come out from behind the clouds to light it so that she might discover some hiding place, a niche in the rocks large enough to conceal herself.

Voices drifted to her, followed by the soft crunch of a boat being drawn up on the shore. Quickly she crouched in the shadows of an overhanging rock and gathered her cloak about her. She saw two figures outlined against the sky. They spoke, but in tones too low for her to hear what was said. One of them carried something. She had just distinguished the shape of a lantern when it flickered into life and was shaded by the man's cloak. She held her breath for a moment, as the figure walked to the water's edge and held the light aloft, and within seconds an answering signal came from the ship. The light vanished and the two figures began to move along the beach towards her hiding place and, to her horror, came to a halt only inches from where she crouched. She had but to reach out a hand and she could have touched the hem of a cloak. It seemed a miracle they couldn't hear her heart pounding and she pressed a hand to her mouth.

'Something's gone wrong,' she heard one say. 'He should have been here.'

'You forget, there's a war, Simmonds. There are spies everywhere. It can't be easy.'

The other grunted. 'No, my lord, but nor is it possible to keep a ship so close into shore. Apart from the risk of being seen there is the tide.'

She heard the sound of one of the men blowing on his hands and chafing them together. Her own were numb with cold yet she daren't move. She saw his profile as he seemed to study the stretch of beach. 'God's teeth, do you think I put the lives of my men at risk without good cause? We have no choice. We must wait until the rendezvous is kept. You know what's at stake.'

'Can you be so sure it will be kept?' came the quiet response, and she heard the other's muttered oath.

'Until I hear with my own ears that the King is dead, I shall continue and so will every other man under my command.'

They were royalists. They spoke of the King. A gasp of joy broke from her involuntarily, sending the men whirling about, and she heard the rasp of a sword being drawn.

'God's teeth, what have we here?'

Her hand flew to her mouth, suppressing a scream. Instinctively she tried to run, but the attempt was doomed to failure from the first. Hampered by her gown, her limbs numbed by the cold and from having crouched in her narrow refuge, she was trapped. Rough hands dragged her upwards and a lantern was held so that its light fell on her face. She tried to turn her head, but one of the men thrust back her hood and swore softly.

'A woman.'

'Women can spy as admirably as any man,' the other hissed, and suddenly his sword point was at her throat. 'She has heard every word.'

She tried to speak, but the sound died in her throat. Her chin was held and her gaze forced upwards. A pair of eyes stared into hers and she managed, somehow, through clenched teeth to cry, 'No, my lord, I am no spy. I swear it.'

He laughed mirthlessly and with sickening dread she realised that his gaze was taking in her gown, revealed as her cloak was wrenched aside in the struggle.

'A Puritan and no spy?'

Verity shivered. 'I can explain . . .'

She heard his soft laughter. 'I'll be bound you can.' Then his tone changed abruptly, 'What are you doing here if not spying?'

'More to the point, how much did she hear?' The tip of the sword wavered threateningly against her throat.

'Unless she is deaf, which she is obviously not, everything.'

'Then we have no choice?' The words fell menacingly into the darkness and only the fact that she was held so tightly prevented her from falling.

She stared helplessly at the man who held her. In the darkness it was impossible to distinguish his features, yet by his voice she knew him to be young. His hair was long and curling, she thought it light in colour. He wore a beard and moustache and she caught the glimpse of lace at his collar.

She guessed him to be a gentleman from the manner of his dress and his voice, yet she didn't doubt that he would kill her without a qualm if he thought it necessary.

The sword wavered and she held her breath. 'It is true, my lord. I did hear. But you must believe that I would never betray you. Far from it, I share your cause.'

'A likely story,' the man Simmonds sneered.

'You may be right. Either way we can take no chances.'

A calculating gaze studied her and she shivered. 'What do you mean to do with me?'

'Your presence seems to present us with a dilemma,' the voice said, coolly. 'The fact that you have witnessed our presence here makes you a danger to us.'

'You . . . you mean to kill me.' Her voice was little more than a whisper.

He studied her in silence for a long moment then smiled. 'On the contrary. You may be of more value to us alive. Mister Simmonds,' the voice rapped. 'The lady will accompany us aboard. We shall discover just how much she knows and perhaps she can tell us other things which may be of value. Put up your sword, man. Our . . . other cargo is obviously delayed. Let's see what we have in its stead.'

Before she could protest she was gathered up unceremoniously and carried in a pair of muscular arms to the small boat where she was dumped aboard. It occurred to her to protest as the craft was pushed away from the beach and Simmonds began to row. She had no idea what awaited her, nor even if she would ever be released. There was something of a nightmare quality about the whole thing, but the futility of argument or of attempting escape was reinforced by the glint of the pistol which was pointed with deadly accuracy at her breast.

The ship rocked gently on the changing tide. There were no lights showing as they drew alongside, the small boat jarring as it made contact. A voice called down to them out of the darkness. Verity felt her arm held as she was jolted forward and tried to rise.

She stared with dismay at the rope ladder. How would she ever climb it hampered by the fullness of her skirts and with the ship moving steadily? She drew back, her eyes wide. 'I . . . I cannot.'

She heard the soft laughter behind her. 'Then allow me to assist.'

With a cry of dismay she was aware of being hoisted off her feet and slung over a hard shoulder so that her head dangled sickeningly towards the waves. She closed her eyes, moaning, beating helplessly at the figure who subjected her to such humiliation. Then other hands held her and she was hauled over the ship's side and found herself standing, albeit unsteadily, upon the deck. She swayed at the unfamiliar rocking movement. Shadowy figures moved. She started as a voice came from behind her and turned quickly to see a frowning face.

'What's this then? A strange cargo, my lord.'

'Not what we expected, but interesting, I suspect,' her captor said in quiet tones.

'You'd best bring her below. Bo'sun, weigh anchor and let's get out of here.'

'Aye, Cap'n, Sir.'

A hand pressed on her shoulder, urging her forward. She obeyed, dry-mouthed, her feet slipping on the sea-washed decks. What if her story was not believed? These men were desperate. They might silence her anyway rather than risk having her betray their presence.

She moved as if in a dream, following the man who must be the captain of the vessel, conscious of her second captor close behind. Her eyes were becoming slowly accustomed to the semi-darkness, but, having no knowledge of ships, she stumbled several times until her arm was held firmly.

They entered a cabin. She was unprepared for the brilliance of a lamp and she flung up a hand, dazzled, as she was pushed forward. The Captain uttered an oath, staring at her and then at her captors.

'In God's name, Wilmot, what have you brought aboard my ship? I thought it was bigger game you were after than some mere girl.'

She was dismayed by the hostility she saw in his tanned, bearded face. He paced the cabin, a tall figure, his muscular arms brown beneath his unlaced shirt and leather doublet. With an angry gesture he rolled up the chart he had been studying earlier and thrust it into one of several studded oak chests, his gaze returning to her.

'It's no game,' the man he had addressed as Wilmot said quietly, and for the first time she looked properly at her captor. He dragged the hat from his head and she saw his long, fair hair flattened damply against his collar. There was exhaustion etched into his young features.

A look passed between the two and she waited, helplessly, as they seemed to be considering the best means of disposing of her.

'The cargo we were expecting didn't arrive, but we came upon this girl instead. Unfortunately, she heard what was said, and, short of killing her, which I had no stomach for, we had no choice but to bring her with us.'

'And what, pray, am I supposed to do with her? Feed her to the fishes?'

She shuddered as they discussed her so coldly. She turned desperately to the Captain. 'I am no spy, you must believe me.'

'A likely story.' He moved closer. She had drawn the hood of her cloak over her head. He thrust it roughly back and she saw his eyes widen momentarily. She could only guess at her appearance, her hair, the bruises.

'You expect me to believe that you were there, alone in the dark, by chance?' he asked bitterly.

She swallowed, shivering with fear as much as cold. Her only chance lay in speaking the truth convincingly, yet the story sounded incredible, even to her own ears. 'It is true that I . . . suspected. I saw what must have been your ship in this cove two nights since. But that was not why I was there tonight. I was not spying.'

He paced round her. 'Nonetheless, you heard

what was said.'

She nodded dumbly, biting at her lip as she stared up at him. 'I would never betray you. I long for the King's safety as much as you do. I despise Cromwell . . .'

His hands grasped violently at her cloak, thrusting it aside as he stared at her gown. 'Fine words.'

Wilmot leaned with deceptive nonchalance against the curved timbers of the ship's cabin. 'I fear you present too great a risk.' She was aware of the pistol in his hand and drew back with a cry. Drymouthed she stared at it and at the men, seeing no pity in their eyes. Her chin rose. 'Very well, if you mean to kill me I can do nothing to prevent it, but at least you must know that you are in grave danger.'

The Captain moved, pushing aside the pistol which was pressed close to her head. He looked closely at her. 'Why do you tell us this? Who are you?'

She was trembling so much that he must be aware of it. 'I am a friend, a royalist, like yourself.'

Doubt narrowed his eyes. 'Then let's see more of this royalist.'

With a cry she felt the cloak ripped from her and the lantern suddenly swung close. She shrank back, only to be held ruthlessly. He stared, releasing his breath slowly as he saw her bruised, naked flesh beneath the torn gown.

'God's teeth, someone has used you cruelly.'

The lantern was lowered quickly. She had forgotten the state of her gown and struggled urgently to cover herself. She was supported with new gentleness to a chair and a glass of wine was pressed into her hands. She sipped it gladly, feeling the warmth revive her.

'Who is responsible for this?'

She closed her eyes, wishing the memory of that nightmare would end.

'Roundheads,' her voice was little more than a whisper. 'Kill me if you must, but I speak the truth, you are in danger if you remain here. There are troopers billeted in my grandfather's house. We had no choice, they came . . .'

Wilmot frowned. 'What is your name, Mistress?'

Her hand rose, shakily, to her brow. 'I am Verity Ashbourne.'

'Ashbourne?' Wilmot's booted foot was lowered from the chair as he stared at her. 'Your father, he was Henry Ashbourne?'

Her brow furrowed. 'No, Sir, that was my uncle who fought with Cromwell's army. My father was Robert Ashbourne. He died at Naseby.'

'Indeed,' came the soft response, 'I had the honour to serve with him there.'

Three pairs of eyes studied her now.

'There is a likeness,' Wilmot's features relaxed. 'He was a fine man. I was proud to serve with him.' He frowned uncomfortably then, 'I regret the manner of your being brought here. Had I known . . .'

'How could you?' she said. 'In any event, perhaps it is as well. You might have walked straight into a trap.'

'You say there are troopers. How many?'

'Perhaps twenty. All roads and bridges are being watched and, I think, this cove. They suspect that fugitives may be heading this way to take ship to France.'

'Damnation,' Wilmot's fist thudded into his palm. The captain watched him uneasily as he poured a glass of wine and downed it in one swallow.

'I can't risk my ship and crew indefinitely. You can't be sure that the cargo you expect will ever arrive.'

Verity glanced uncertainly from one to the other. 'If the cargo is what I believe it to be, then you may still have hope.' For a moment she feared she had spoken recklessly as Wilmot's expression grew taut, then she recognised that if they wished to kill her they could easily do so. Nothing was to be gained by her silence now. 'There has been no word of the King's capture, and if he had been taken, we must have heard of it.'

'You are indeed your father's daughter, Mistress Ashbourne,' Wilmot's glance of admiration confused her and she looked away.

'I am not very brave, my lord, but I believe, as you do, that England's one hope for the future lies with the King. My fear is that he will walk unknowingly into danger. The troops are alert, they suspect something, otherwise they would not have come to Kingswood.'

The Captain stirred, his features gaunt in the light of the taper he used to ignite his clay pipe. 'I have my crew to think of as well as my ship. If the roads and bridges are being watched this entire stretch of coast must also be under observation. Each day's delay adds to the danger of our being discovered.'

'He will come,' Wilmot insisted quietly. 'You can't give up now, man. You realise what it will mean if he should get this far only to find he is abandoned to his enemies? He *will* come.'

'I'm as loyal as you are, my lord, but I'm also a

practical man. The tides won't wait even for Charles Stuart.'

Verity listened in silence, exhaustion sweeping over her. She was becoming increasingly afraid that her absence from the house would be noted and the alarm raised.

'Let me go,' she said suddenly. 'I can keep watch, listen to what is said and warn you.'

'Or betray us,' the Captain's eyes narrowed.

'If I had wished to betray you, I could have done so when I first saw your ship.'

'Then why did you not?'

She shrugged wearily. Despair seemed to embolden her somehow and she looked at him directly. 'If you believe I am a traitor to your cause then you must do with me as you wish. I can only give you my word. My father was given a chance to prove his loyalty. I ask only the same.'

'Even if it means that in so doing, you may also die?'

'Even so,' she said, sharply.

Wilmot nodded, frowning. He glanced at the Captain. 'She is right. You say yourself that we hazard not only the ship but the entire mission if our presence is discovered, yet somehow we must be ready to move swiftly when the time comes.'

'Your contact was to have had his cargo here by now.'

Wilmot's hand rose. 'It can't be easy to travel with troopers all over the countryside. He's delayed, that's all.'

Verity drew in her breath and closed her eyes as she listened. The stale air of the cabin seemed to be closing in upon her, the steady movement of the ship drugging her senses, adding to a feeling of unreality. She brushed a hand weakly against her brow and started suddenly as Edward Wilmot spoke. She opened her eyes to feel his hand gently upon her arm, the other proffering a glass of wine.

'Come, drink this.'

With trembling hands she took it and sipped at it. 'I fear I shall be missed and if a search is made . . .'

He was drawing her cloak more firmly about her. The Captain issued some murmured order to a member of his crew. 'You will be put ashore, Mistress Ashbourne.'

Her eyes widened. 'You mean that you will trust me?'

'I don't think it will be misplaced,' Wilmot replied gently, 'but there will be danger.'

She shrugged, trying not to think of Richard Kingston and what he would do were he to discover her betrayal. Holding her cloak about her she was led from the cabin and back to the deck. She was glad of the cold air, feeling it revive her. She could hear the timbers creaking with the steady movement of the ship. There were no lights on deck, but in the moonlight she could see figures moving in response to the Captain's commands. He stared up at the sky, his hand gripping the rigging.

'I don't like this light. It's too bright, we could be seen from the shore. I'm taking her to cover.'

It was on the tip of her tongue to ask where a vessel of this size could be hidden, then she bit back the question. It was better that she did not know such things.

She held back the strands of hair which were whipped across her face by the wind as she turned to Wilmot.

'How shall I reach you if I have news?'

He leaned against the side rail, staring into the rising swell of the water below. 'Can you signal from the cliff top?'

She considered, frowning. 'It would be dangerous. There is always the risk of someone else, perhaps someone from the house, seeing. I can't be sure whether there are troopers in the woods.'

'More than likely there are. You may be seen yourself.'

'Maybe so,' she replied, frankly. 'But I have not been confined to the house as yet. I can usually manage to slip away and if I leave a lantern hidden somewhere in the cove . . .' She frowned. 'But what of you? The cove may be under observation, surely?'

'That is a risk we must take. If you signal once for danger we shall keep off. Signal twice and we shall know you have news and it is safe to come ashore.'

She nodded, then she was being helped over the side of the ship, staring for one terrifying moment into the dark waters. Her numbed fingers clung to the rope ladder as her feet searched for a hold, then strong arms reached up to catch her about the waist and she was set down in the small boat again.

The man began to row for the shore. She stared at the ship, looking for the figure at the rail, but he was already swallowed up in the darkness. The boat bumped gently against the shingle. She rose and the man leapt out to help her ashore, then, before she could begin to thank him, he was already pushing the craft away and she was left alone.

Pausing only for a moment to gain her bearings, she bent her head against the wind and hurried towards the cliff path. She was trembling as she reached the top and turned to stare out to sea. The ship was gone and she suddenly felt alone and defenceless. If she was caught she knew that she could expect no mercy from Captain Richard Kingston.

The hem of her cloak was heavy where a layer of damp sand clung to it and her hair straggled darkly against her face as she broke from the cover of the woods and ran towards the house. Lamps glowed at the windows and she could imagine her aunt and cousin seated before the fire with their stitching.

Then a quiver of alarm ran through her and she drew to a halt, pressing closer to the wall. Two unfamiliar horses were tethered before the steps of the house. She pondered on the reason that could bring yet more visitors to Kingswood as she entered stealthily by the servant's entrance and made her way quickly to her room.

She gasped as a figure detached itself from the shadows of her bedchamber, then released her breath slowly as Meg's features became clearer in the light from the window. She stifled an urge to rebuke the old woman for her habit of lurking soundlessly, then bit back the words as she leaned, breathlessly, for a moment against the door. On this occasion at least she was relieved to find Meg waiting.

'Draw the curtains, quickly, and light the lamp,' she ordered. 'Then help me out of these wet things.'

The old woman moved to her task unhurriedly, muttering beneath her breath. 'Where have you been? I've been watching for you this past hour and you nowhere to be found.' As the pale glow of light flooded the room her old eyes narrowed with shock before she moved to push aside Verity's fumbling fingers and herself unfastened the torn gown and muddied cloak. They fell to the floor, leaving the girl's figure naked. Her wizened fingers probed the dark bruises and she sucked in her breath sharply.

'This looks like the work of the devil.'

'Don't question me now,' Verity begged. 'Just swear you'll say nothing and hurry, bring me a fresh gown.' She stepped from the folds of the discarded one and took the other which Meg lifted from the linen chest, holding aside her hair as the old woman struggled with the fastenings, then she reached for a brush and began to run it through the heavy strands of her hair.

'Has my aunt been asking for me?'

The old woman's mouth twisted. 'Not she. She's had other things to occupy her mind. Strangers came this late noon.'

Verity's hand tightened about the brush. 'Who are they? What do they want here?'

Meg stared at the girl's reflection in the glass. 'They are Commissioners.'

Verity half-turned, her face white. 'You mean Cromwell's Commissioners?'

'Who else,' came the bitter response.

A pulse hammered violently in Verity's throat. 'What do they want here?'

'You think they would tell me? I only know they were asking for you. They spoke with the Captain, then spent near an hour questioning your grandfather.'

An angry flush darkened Verity's cheeks. 'I must go to him.' The words were barely audible. Her reflection in the glass shocked her as she saw the whiteness of her face and the bruise now showing quite clearly across her temple. Her lips were still swollen and, closing her eyes for a moment, a vision of Richard Kingston swam so clearly into her mind that she swayed. She opened her eyes quickly and drew herself up. So far it was he who held all the power, but now at last she had the means of exacting revenge. The day would come when Captain Richard Kingston would pay with his life for the things he had done. She had only to watch and listen.

The thought should have filled her with joy, yet, suddenly, it was as if the fires of hatred died within her, leaving her inexplicably cold and trembling.

'I must go to my grandfather.' At the door she paused. 'Don't worry, Meg. Some day, soon, God willing, this nightmare will be over and we shall be free.'

CHAPTER
SIX

BUT it was less easy to believe her own words as she stood before the great oak desk in the library with Commissioner Thomas Thurloe's piercing gaze fixed upon her. Until now she had only heard of such men—seen in the flesh, the reality was far more terrifying. As if aware of her nervousness, the man came round the desk to pace before her, his steely gaze directed at her down-bent head.

Short of stature, he was clad entirely in black, from the hat he swept off his head to reveal the hideously short-cropped hair, to his jacket and breeches. Her lowered gaze watched with chill fascination the progress of his square-toed shoes across the floor, beating out an echoing tattoo. Above it his voice rolled thunderously. Everything about him bespoke the fanatic and an icy hand seemed to grip her spine.

She longed to sit, but he had kept her standing purposely, by so doing adding subtly to her feelings of vulnerability. In another man lack of height might have robbed him of such advantage. In Thomas Thurloe a burning fanaticism banished any notions of weakness even before they rose in her numbed brain. He was a dangerous man. She resisted the urge to follow his movements with her eyes as he studied her. A flush began to creep up her neck as his gaze seemed to linger on the stray wisps of golden hair which had escaped from beneath her cap, her figure whose curves not even the drab, grey gown could disguise.

The footsteps ceased and her glance rose involuntarily. In that split second in which their eyes met she surprised in him a look which held so little of the virtues his Puritan manner professed that she recoiled in horror. His gaze flickered and when it lifted again he was in control, but an awareness added to her fear and she clasped her hands together until the knuckles were white in an effort not to betray their trembling.

'How long have you lived in this house, Mistress Ashbourne?'

She started as his voice broke the silence. Why should he wish to know of such things? In a large, high-back chair another man sat writing. Tobias Hammond frowned and looked up, pen poised.

'Answer, Mistress.'

'All my life. I was born here,' she said in a low voice. What did Cromwell's Commissioners want with her?

'Your father was a royalist,' an angry flush darkened his thick-set features.

In spite of her fear a sense of hatred for such bigoted intolerance made her lift her head and face him directly. 'He fought for his King. His annointed Sovereign whom he was sworn to serve.'

Thomas Thurloe moved closer and her nerves felt tensed almost to snapping point. She looked about her desperately, knowing there was no escape. The tall figure blocking the doorway regarded her with contempt and she lowered her lashes, veiling her hatred of Richard Kingston. She was unaware that it was conveyed admirably in the stricken pallor of her face, and his mouth grew taut.

Thomas Thurloe stood behind her. She felt her scalp tingle as if it were the Devil himself, and longed to put some distance between herself and her tormenter.

'You were right, Captain,' he murmured. 'You did well to warn us of this dissenter in our midst.'

Her eyes widened with horror as she stared at her betrayer, her heart pounding fiercely. It seemed she had made the mistake of under-estimating her enemy yet again. Her hands clenched until the nails bit into her palms with a desire for revenge, yet his gaze locked with hers, unmoved, and she was sickened by his ruthlessness.

Her questioner moved to sit at the edge of the desk. She stood very still, trying to regain control of her emotions. Whatever it was they wanted of her, she would not make it easy.

'You spend a great deal of time in the company of your grandfather.'

It was a statement, not a question. She swallowed hard, longing for a drink to rid her of the dryness in her throat.

'I see no sin in that. We are kin. He has cared for me . . .'

'You consider yourself a judge of what is sinful, Mistress?' Thomas Thurloe said contemptuously.

She moistened her lips with her tongue. 'He is an old man who dreams dreams and likes to talk of the past.'

His eyes narrowed. 'And of what do you talk?'

Panic rose. 'Of many things. There is no harm in it.'

His lips curved into a sneer. 'The Devil speaks through old and young alike. I have heard his voice come out of the mouth of a babe in the cradle and it is a loathesome sight, Mistress. When a spirit is possessed by such evil there is but one remedy. It must be driven out by fire, for the Devil never willingly relinquishes a soul.'

She swayed, sickened by such fervour. But she must not faint. She must not let them think her afraid or weak.

'Of what does the old man talk?' the voice rapped again.

Her own seemed to answer from far away, sounding strangely calm, 'Of the days my grand-father spent at court as a young man.'

'And of the King, no doubt?'

A pulse hammered in her throat. 'Perhaps.' She pressed a hand to her brow. 'Many things, I cannot remember.'

'But there is no longer a King, Mistress Ash-bourne, merely a traitor who styles himself thus.'

Incredibly she felt the laughter bubble up to her lips as she faced him. 'You speak of Master Crom-well, Sir, why then I must believe you.'

Vaguely she heard the sharp intake of breath and was aware of Richard Kingston's sudden move-ment towards her before his hand rose. Her head reeled under the force of the blow as she staggered, gasping with pain. As she fell he towered over her and she was aware of the dark eyes staring menac-ingly down into hers. Thomas Thurloe's distorted features loomed and receded before hands came down to grip her arm and Richard Kingston's face was close to her own.

'That was unwise, Mistress,' he hissed, 'very unwise.'

'Get her to her feet,' Thomas Thurloe's voice had risen to a strange pitch. His face was grey with fury as she was dragged upwards and stood unsteadily, a hand clutched to her cheek. 'You are aware that the penalty for treason is death?'

Her head was throbbing unmercifully. 'I have done nothing.'

'You make no pretence of your royalist sympathies and allow yourself to be encouraged in such beliefs.'

Goaded by fear and helplessness she stared at him. 'Of what are you afraid? Of myself? Of an old man who is near blind and too weak to leave his room? Are these your enemies? Then there is little danger for you here.' Tears hung on her lashes as she lowered her head, despising him for the gleam of triumph she saw in his eyes. He mistook it for submission.

'It is as well that you recognise that you can never win. It would be foolish even to try. In a short time Charles Stuart will be taken and will pay the penalty for his crimes.'

She kept her head lowered, afraid he would see the new wariness which suddenly sprang to her eyes. He spoke with such certainty. What was the real reason for his presence here?

'Go now,' he ordered, 'and pray that your immortal soul might be saved.'

She moved as if in a dream and, as he spoke again, paused at the door. He was addressing the Captain, and she made a pretence of releasing the heel of her shoe from the hem of her gown. 'The Lord Protector regrets your absence from his side in London, Captain. Three months is a long time and His Highness has need of men like you about him.'

She saw the smile flicker on Richard Kingston's lips. 'This war is not over yet. When it is I shall be pleased to return.'

For one moment his glance locked with hers and she shuddered.

'There will be a place of honour for you, Captain. His Highness rewards those who serve him well.'

'The only honour I care for is that of bringing the traitor Charles Stuart to London as my prisoner.'

'An endeavour which God will surely hasten to assist.' Thomas Thurloe drew him closer to the fire. 'I am to tell you that extra troops will be here within a few days. His Highness wishes an end to this war. It can only truly be achieved when the Stuart is dealt with.'

Verity straightened, conscious of a sense of helpless dread. She saw Richard Kingston bow his acknowledgement of the words before he raised a glass to his lips. She fled blindly, the tears coursing down her cheeks, the bitter taste of fear in her mouth. Somehow she would see him denied his victory, no matter what the cost.

She entered her grandfather's room to find him lying propped against the pillows in his great bed. His eyes were closed, his face ashen. A candle flickered on the table beside him and in the pale circle of light his face seemed so grotesquely thin that she knew an instant of alarm.

Jacob Reymes straightened up in his task of adding logs to the fire to regard her arrival with pleasure. She stood at the door, afraid to approach the bed for fear of what she might find. Her grandfather lay so still, the skin of his hands paper-thin as they lay on the coverlet.

'What have they done to him?'

Reymes shook his head, wiping his hands upon

the faded velvet of his doublet. 'They questioned him very harshly. I tried to prevent it, but the man Thurloe has authority. To have tried to thwart him might have been more dangerous.'

She crossed slowly towards the bed and took one of the frail hands in her own, feeling the thready pulse. 'We are all helpless against them.'

'I fear for Sir John's health,' Reymes murmured, gathering up a tray. 'This war has hit him hard and now he must see parliament troops billeted in this very house.'

Her mouth compressed in rare bitterness as she stared at the figure in the bed. 'How did parliament ever come to have so much power and the King to lose it?' she whispered. 'My father once told me that the King dissolved parliament and ruled well enough without them and their mischief-making.'

'They knew he could not survive for ever without them. They had but to wait, and they were right. There was the war with the Scottish Covenanters— the King had no means of raising the money. He had no choice but to recall them and that, in the eyes of many, was the beginning of the end.'

The sleeping figure stirred, roused by their voices, and she blinked away her tears. 'Grandfather, it is Verity.'

She saw confusion and then alarm mirrored in his eyes. 'They haven't harmed you, child?'

'No, no, Grandfather,' she offered the quick reassurance, glad that he could not see the anger glittering in her eyes. 'But I am afraid. These men are not here by chance. They have some special purpose, something which concerns the King.'

She heard his swift intake of breath. 'What are you saying, child?'

'I believe they are setting a trap. There was talk of more troopers coming and if they do we are lost, the King is lost.' She was unaware of the flush in her cheeks as she spoke with such vehemence, or of the quick flicker of alarm in Jacob Reymes's eyes as he moved closer. 'Grandfather, there is a ship in the cove. A royalist ship.'

She was shocked by the sudden anger which had her grandfather trying to rise from his bed. 'In pity's name, child, have you dared disobey me? Did I not ask for your word? What have you been meddling in?'

Protesting, she tried to restrain him only to find herself thrust aside. Disbelieving, she stared at him. 'You don't know what you are asking.'

'You have not the least notion of what you are getting involved in.'

She drew a breath, trying to still the fit of trembling that had overtaken her. 'I am no longer a child, Grandfather. How can I not become involved in something which affects the lives of us all so deeply. Please, don't ask me to stand aside and do nothing. How could I think myself worthy of the name royalist if I stood by . . . ?'

To her dismay he thrust her aside and began to get out of bed. 'Dear God, if I but had my sight.'

'What are you doing?' She watched helplessly as he reached for the support of Jacob Reymes's arm.

'Somehow I mean to prevent what you are trying to do.'

She gasped with horror. 'I am doing what must be done. How can I make you understand?' Her face was deathly white. 'There is a ship waiting to carry the King to safety and in this very house there are men who mean to take him prisoner and bring him to trial. You know what that will mean?' Her voice was little more than a whisper. 'Cromwell will not feel safe until the King is beheaded as his father before him. Someone *must* warn them.'

'Child, you must believe me, there are things you don't understand.'

Her mouth compressed rebelliously. 'I beg you do not try to stop me, for I should hate above all things to have to disobey you. I can get word to the men aboard that ship. There may be time to warn the King. He must not come here.'

His frail fingers caught at her wrist with surprising strength. 'I forbid you.'

Even as she protested she became aware with a sense of horror that they were no longer alone. Richard Kingston stood in the open doorway, surveying the scene, his dark eyes glinting with anger. She could only stare at him in blank dismay. How much had he heard? In a few strides he had crossed the room and before she knew what he intended she found herself in his grasp, his hands biting into the flesh of her arms as he shook her remorselessly.

'You little fool. What must I do to teach you obedience? Thus far I have been lenient. I see it was a mistake.'

She gasped at the ruthlessness she saw in his face and tried, in vain, to wrench herself free of his grasp. She struck out furiously with her free hand until that too was caught and twisted behind her.

'Let me go.'

His lips were tight-set with malice as he stared down at her, her body strained close against his own. 'Let you go, Mistress? That you may practise more treason?' came the savage response. 'You were warned that I could be a dangerous enemy.'

She sobbed as his arm went swiftly about her waist and she was lifted, struggling, from her feet. Her hands beat blindly at him and once again his strength amazed her. She was vaguely aware of her grandfather clinging helplessly to Jacob Reymes for support, his face ashen as he watched, unable to come to her aid. Blazing eyes stared warningly down into hers and she sagged weakly in her captor's arms, unable to fight any longer.

'I hate you,' the blood had drained from her face leaving it deathly pale. Above her, his face contorted grimly.

'Your hatred does not trouble me, but your obedience does, and I mean to have it.' His glance flickered meaningfully towards her grandfather and she felt suddenly sick with fear. 'If you give me any further trouble, I shall make you regret it.'

'You would not dare,' she whispered. 'Are you so cowardly that you must fight your war against old men?'

'I will do whatever is necessary, and it is not wise to dare me, Mistress Ashbourne. I mean to be master here, as you will learn to your cost, if you persist. I have been gentle so far.'

Her eyes blazed with angry humiliation. 'Gentle? You are a savage.'

His voice was soft, yet the threat was there. 'I can do far worse.' His arm tightened about her and in one swift movement they were out of the room. She stood within the circle of his arms feeling the sense of despair and frustration sweep over her. She was helpless, bound not only by his strength but by those other emotions which also threatened to consume her. Suddenly his lips were against her cheek. She moaned involuntarily as, for an instant, the

cruel pressure of his hands was released and he
moulded her body ruthlessly to his own. His cares-
ses were gentle yet insistent and she abandoned
herself to them with a wildness which held her as if
she was drowning in a whirlpool of ecstasy. His
mouth moved from her lips to the hair he released
roughly from its cap to send spilling like a shower of
gold over her shoulders and his voice murmured
softly against her cheek.

'Trust me.'

The words broke the spell. She froze in his arms
and with a cry of horror wrenched herself from his
grasp. Trust him? Her green eyes were filled with
contempt as she stared at him. What madness had
almost caused her to forget who and what he was?

She was dimly aware as she turned and fled, of his
face, contorted by some expression which she could
not read and dare not wait to discover. As she ran,
sobbing, she pressed a hand to her mouth as if to
wipe away the pressure of that kiss. She had been
right to call him a savage. He knew nothing of
conscience and now she had given him the very
means by which to betray them.

CHAPTER
SEVEN

THAT night seemed the longest Verity had ever endured. She tossed and turned until the first pale light of dawn began to creep in through the curtains, then, abandoning all pretence at sleep, she got out of bed.

When Margaret came to wake her as usual an hour later, it was to find her already dressed and staring thoughtfully out of the window. Her eyes seemed larger in the paleness of her face and there was a new purposefulness about her. Daylight had brought no escape from despair. Her grandfather was still a hostage, they were both at the mercy of Richard Kingston. Through the hours of darkness she had become more and more aware of the dangers which threatened, yet, in spite of them, she knew that she must not let her resolution waver.

Her gaze sought the clock. It was early yet and the day stretched interminably ahead. She turned as Margaret set down the tray, and something in the old woman's expression filled her with a new sense of foreboding.

'What is wrong? What has happened?'

'Wrong? Master Thurloe is conducting an inspection of the house with Mistress Ashbourne, that's what's wrong, and your aunt behaving as if she is mistress here.'

'I don't understand. For what purpose . . . ?'

Margaret began to strip back the bedcovers with angry movements, muttering under her breath, 'Apparently there are changes to be made.'

The girl's eyes widened with alarm. 'Changes? But my aunt has no right. This is my grandfather's house.'

The old woman shrugged. 'I only know I'm ordered to take down the pictures.'

Verity's hands clenched in sudden anger. 'But she can't do it. Many of those pictures were part of my grandmother's dower, brought with her when she came from France to wed my grandfather. He treasures them.'

'Aye, well, I only know what I'm told,' came the tight response. 'And French means Papist. It seems that Master Thurloe's word is to be heard now in this house, and who am I to argue with one of Master Cromwell's commissioners?'

Verity stared, feeling the wave of angry resentment surge over her.

'No, you must do as you are bid,' she said quietly, and as she went quickly to her grandfather's room a new determination was already taking root.

He was waiting for her and she knew from the look on his face that he had heard what was happening.

'Can you do nothing to stop them,' she cried desperately, only to see the answer already in his eyes.

'What is to be done?' he shook his head. 'No, child, let them have their way. After all, it is only pictures they destroy.'

She gasped. 'But they were my grandmother's. You have treasured them.'

'And shall continue to treasure their memory,

but she would not have wished that blood be shed over them.'

Verity's fists clenched helplessly. 'They find sin in everything.'

'Then pity them.'

'Pity? I hate them.'

He shook his head. 'Pictures were not the only legacy your grandmother left.'

She stared at him. 'What do you mean?'

He ran a hand through his beard. 'I mean that there are things they cannot touch.' She watched, bemused, as he signalled to Reymes and the man crossed to the window. He pushed aside the curtain and to her astonishment she saw him run his fingers over the panelling beside it. She heard a gentle click and a small section flew open. From it he drew a bundle of papers, discoloured with age, which he carried to Sir John.

She stared, uncomprehending, as he lifted them. 'Lands.' His voice held a hint of triumph. 'Your grandmother had wealth in her own right. She was to have brought this to me, as part of her dower, but I had no need of it. It was her wish, our wish, that her estates go to our first-born grandchild.' He tried to define her features. 'These are yours. Some day, if ever the need should arise, you can make a new start in France, live safely until England finds its sanity again.'

Her heart was thudding violently within her breast. 'But I could not go. I know nothing of France.'

'There are many exiles there and the numbers increase as every month passes. You must do as they do, wait and work for better times. At least this offers hope and a means.' He handed the papers to Reymes who returned them to their hiding place. 'There is also a little gold, and a ring which was your mother's.'

Verity could not speak, but he clasped her hand and patted it.

'What are a few pictures? Are *we* so easily destroyed?' He smiled, 'Go now, or your aunt will be searching for you.'

Obediently she rose, but her anger remained as she went slowly down the stairs and returned to her room. The old woman was still there, waiting.

'Meg, there is something I must do. Something which may well put us all in grave danger.' She watched, warily, and saw the shrewd old eyes narrow. She was taking a risk, but it had to be done.

'I'm too old to be afraid for myself,' came the quick response.

Verity took the gnarled hands in hers. 'I cannot tell you everything, for your own sake. The less you know the less danger to yourself and to others if you should be questioned. But I can tell you that it concerns the safety of someone of importance to England.' Her teeth caught at her lip. 'This person's safety is of vital importance, but there are men— men like Thomas Thurloe and Richard Kingston— who would prevent his escape.'

Meg's hand came down over hers, silencing further explanation. 'Only tell me what I'm to do. I'd be glad to see an end to their kind.'

'Bless you. I knew I could trust you.'

'Trust me, indeed,' came the sharp response. 'Did I not see you come into this world and hold your hand when you took your first steps?' Her face clouded. 'But there are risks in what you intend . . .'

Green eyes stared imploringly into hers. 'Don't you see, I have to do what I can. Grandfather has tried to dissuade me, but I cannot stand by and watch Richard Kingston set his trap.' She went quickly to the window, pushing it open so that the breeze swept over her cheeks before she turned to the woman again. 'It is vital that I get out of this house tonight. I know it will not be easy, but I must warn someone, someone who is a good friend, that more troops are due to arrive and that a trap is being set.' She shivered, 'With or without your help I mean to go, Meg.'

She saw the expression which darkened the old woman's face.

'As if you ever needed any blessing of mine.' The look of concern in the old eyes belied the sharpness of her tone.

'You know how dear you are to me.'

'Aye.' Suddenly embarrassed, Meg's hand flapped her away. 'Well have I not already said you shall have my help?'

A sigh of relief passed Verity's lips and she realised that she was trembling.

'I may be gone for several hours and it is vital that no one should know.'

'If anyone should question your whereabouts I shall say you have gone to bed suffering from a slight fever.'

'I must be able to get back into the house when everyone else has retired.'

'Then I shall slip back the bolt when the house is quiet. But if Sir John should find out . . .'

'He must never know.'

'Unless you are caught.'

But that was a prospect she could not allow herself even to think on. The whole thing was already too much like a nightmare. If she allowed her courage to waver one jot it might fail her altogether and too much depended upon her actions. The thought of a future governed by men like Thomas Thurloe was too abhorrent. She pushed it away and rose to her feet.

'I must go and tend to my duties. No one must suspect that this day is any different from the rest.'

But as she made her way downstairs it was to discover that things were already different. It was impossible not to see the gaps left by the pictures which had been removed from the walls. In the hall a similar sight greeted her and she stared in dismayed anger at the brighter patches where the familiar pictures had hung for nearly half a century.

She dashed away the tears as Prudence approached. It seemed as if, in deference to the Commissioners' presence, her cousin had donned her plainest gown, unrelieved even by white collar and cuffs, and the yellow curls, so seductively displayed for the Captain's benefit, were now modestly concealed by linen cap.

Verity's glance went from her cousin to the carelessly stacked pictures.

'Why has this been done? By whose authority?'

Prudence's mouth pursed unattractively. 'One's mind should not be diverted from Godly thoughts. The vanity of possession is wicked. *They* are wicked. Mama has ordered them to be burned.'

Verity stared at the girl who seemed suddenly a stranger. 'Master Thurloe must find you an apt pupil. You repeat his words so well. It is a pity he lacks that very charity his faith is said to profess.'

Prudence's face whitened before her gaze rose

spitefully. 'It is you who will soon learn the meaning of charity, cousin.'

Verity drew in her breath. Nothing was to be gained by arguing and she made no attempt to detain Prudence, but anger burned in her at the thought of such needless destruction as the burning of those pictures. Unable to stem her tears she fled from the house.

The weather had changed during the night and as she crossed the yard the faint smell of sea-mist crept up to her nostrils. She breathed it in deeply. This house which she had loved all her life had become like a prison, a prison from which there could be no escape, and she hated the man who was responsible for making it so.

In the yard the troopers were going about their daily business. Horses were being led from the stables, harness jingling. Several of the men glanced in her direction and she quickened her steps towards the dairy. The chill air revived her as she poured milk into a pitcher and carried it back to the house. Then she drew back as figures emerged suddenly to come hurrying down the steps. It was Thomas Thurloe and his companion, both wearing black cloaks and high-brimmed hats. The Commissioner stared about him, his breath fanning white into the air, then she held her breath as she saw the Captain approach. He moved with familiar arrogance and she was made aware yet again of his strength and height.

Pressed against the wall she watched as the three spoke together. After a moment a trooper led two horses forward and the commissioners mounted. To her dismay she realised they were leaving. Foolishly she had not anticipated that it would be so soon. It could only mean that the extra troops of which Thomas Thurloe had spoken would be here so much the sooner.

The mist, rolling in grey, muffling clouds, added to her feelings of unease. There was no time to be lost. Somehow she must get to the ship, and quickly. She bit her lip, then became aware of the Captain's dark gaze as he stared, frowning, in her direction. As he seemed to hesitate she gathered up her skirts with her free hand and hurried towards the house. Some instinct made her glance back. To her dismay, he still stood there, watching. What was it about him, she wondered, that always made her feel he knew her every thought, anticipated her every move?

With a sense of despair she knew that even to attempt to reach the cove without the cover of darkness would be utter folly, yet every hour's delay put the lives of those men and their intended passenger at greater risk. Somehow, she must escape.

By noon a freshening breeze had blown away the mists and brought in its place a chilling rain. Glad of the tasks which kept her hands occupied, she paused to stare unhappily from the window at the rising storm and wondered how the men aboard the waiting ship would fare. Many a ship had been blown onto the rocks along this stretch of the coast.

A band of fear tightened about her forehead. As her hand rose to soothe it a movement in the yard below caused her to draw in her breath. Richard Kingston's dark, brooding gaze locked with her own. His hair was lashed damply against his brow, his dark cloak whipped against his boots. She drew back, shakily. He had set himself as a guard upon her, as if, once again, he had guessed her intent and meant to prevent it. Her knees were trembling as she backed away. When she looked out later he was gone and she laughed at her fears. He was trying to frighten her and had succeeded. His very presence was sufficient to set her blood racing and her nerves taut. But she must not be deterred from what she had to do.

By late afternoon darkness was already drawing in and she went about the house lighting the lamps and closing the curtains. Within an hour it would be fully dark. Fear made her actions clumsy, drawing a reprimand from her aunt, but neither she nor Prudence were paying any real attention to her presence. It was as she moved to close the shutters that she saw the shadow where the light fell against the barn, and her blood ran cold. How could she have imagined that a man like Richard Kingston would give up so easily? Betraying no sign that she was aware of his presence, she closed the shutters and turned to her aunt.

'I have a headache. I should like to go to my room, if you have no further need of me?'

As she had expected her aunt showed little interest and moments later she was hurrying to her room where, with Margaret's help, she donned a black cloak.

The old woman's face was lined with concern as she drew the hood over the girl's hair. 'I am afraid for you. The Captain is no fool. If you should be caught . . .'

Verity thrust aside the argument. It was too late now for turning back, even though her nerves were stretched close to breaking point. 'I have no choice. Tomorrow may be too late.'

'He will show you no mercy. That one has the cruelty of the Devil.'

Verity's hands clenched tight. 'When I have done what must be done, it does not matter what he does with me.'

'You say that easily,' Margaret muttered, 'but you know nothing of a man like that.'

Verity was glad of the hood which shaded her face as she turned quickly to gather up the lantern. Her green eyes were dull and there were shadows beneath them. She was only too well aware what he was capable of and for a moment her resolution weakened. She stared bleakly into the woman's eyes and was held close until she released herself quickly, afraid that she might be persuaded. 'Save your arguments,' her brows drew together then as she paused and crossed to a casket which stood on a table beside the bed. From it she drew a dagger, its hilt elaborate, the blade cruel. Her mind rebelled at the thought that she might be forced to use it. Would she have either the courage or the strength if the need arose? Quickly she concealed it in the folds of her skirt and gathered her cloak about her.

'Keep this door locked until I return. If anyone should ask for me you have given me a sleeping draught to ease the headache and you cannot rouse me. You understand?' Pausing at the door to be sure her instructions were obeyed, she heard the click of the key in the lock before she began to hurry, her breath drawn in sharply as the chill air of the yard met her.

She stood stock still for a moment, allowing her eyes to become accustomed to the dark. The pale glow of the lights from the house spilled across the open space of the yard and she waited, her eyes searching the shadows. Nothing moved. No sound except the pounding of her own heart. Keeping close to the wall she edged her way clear of the house. She had gone only a few yards when, to her dismay, voices broke the silence and the door of the stable was swung noisily open, trapping her in a beam of light. Frozen with horror she watched as two brawling figures came hurtling towards her, grappling in the mud at her feet. Within seconds other troopers emerged, urging the sparring pair on, shouting and jeering. Pressed against the wall she heard the oaths come from the two men and could only watch helplessly, then her heart went cold as she saw Richard Kingston come striding angrily from the stable. She closed her eyes, willing herself not to faint. Her hand closed about the dagger, knowing that if she were discovered now she would have no explanation for her presence here. He stood, framed in the doorway. His jacket had been abandoned and she saw his muscular shoulders beneath the fabric of his shirt. His head jerked up and for one incredible moment it was as if he stared directly at her. Her throat ached with terror as she waited, then a hand fell on her arm and even as she began to scream another was clasped firmly over her mouth and she was dragged effortlessly away.

'Do not make a sound,' the voice urged, and her reeling senses registered something familiar about him, that here was someone who meant her no harm. She nodded and was released. Her mouth was dry as she tried to speak and the rugged figure loomed more clearly before her.

'Oh Tom, thank God it is you.'

The groom drew her into the shadows of the

barn. 'I'm sorry, mistress, I handled you a mite roughly, but I saw what happened and guessed you had good reason for not wishing to be seen.'

He held the door cracked open and she peered out, frowning. 'I cannot explain, Tom, but I must get away.'

'Tell me what I can do,' came the firm response, and her eyes glistened in the darkness with unshed tears.

'What I need is time. A chance to get away unseen.' She stared helplessly at the brawling figures.

'Then you shall have it. Give me a few seconds.'

She could only watch, bewildered, as the groom disappeared into the darkness and moments later she heard the crackling of hay. She stiffened in alarm. 'Tom, where are you?' There was no answer and she was becoming alarmed when he reappeared, rubbing his hands, to urge her towards the door.

'You'll be safe enough now.'

She frowned as he held open the door then her hand went to her throat as, suddenly, Richard Kingston turned and with an oath, took a step in her direction.

She screamed hoarsely. Her eyes widened desperately and then, from somewhere, came a cry of 'fire'. She coughed as the stench of smoke filled her nostrils and stung at her eyes, then with rapt fascination she saw the swirling clouds of smoke pouring from the barn. Within seconds it was ablaze. She could not move until the voice broke her stunned reverie.

'Go now, Mistress, for pity's sake, go while you can.'

Forcing her numbed limbs into action she picked up her skirts and fled without a backward glance. Only dimly was she aware of the sudden shouts; the running feet as, brawl forgotten, the men became alive to the danger. For a moment she hesitated. Sparks shot into the air as dry hay caught and within seconds, fanned by the wind, became an inferno. The acrid smell filled her throat. She flung up a hand protectively then heard her name called. From out of the curling smoke Richard Kingston moved menacingly towards her.

She ran, scarcely aware of the icy wind whipping across her face, dragging her skirts against her legs. It seemed an eternity before she dared to stop and look back and saw the glow rising to light the sky before she plunged on again. She was shaking with fear, yet, somehow, the fear was not for herself as she heard the distant shouts and remembered the searing heat of the flames into which she had last seen Richard Kingston run.

Her feet unerringly found the tracks through the wood, even in darkness. Briars caught at her skirts as she ran, pausing occasionally to listen and to gain her breath. But if there were troopers posted she neither saw nor heard any hint of their presence.

Looking back once, briefly, in the direction of the house she stifled a gasp of horror at the glow which filled the sky and the smoke, pluming upwards. She could still faintly hear the men's voices raised in alarm, then she shivered and began to move on. This was no time to linger when at any minute she feared to hear Richard Kingston in pursuit.

Reaching the cliff path she began the scramble downwards, feeling the breath burn into her lungs.

The moon was hidden behind cloud and the ground was damp, making her descent more hazardous than usual. Several times her feet slipped on the crumbling track and she only managed to prevent herself from falling by flinging out her hands and clutching desperately at the undergrowth.

She was about halfway down when her foot caught in the hem of her gown and she fell, crying out as pain seared through her ankle. In vain she tried to find some hand-hold, but here the under-growth had given way to rock and sand. Blind panic gripped her as she slid for what seemed an eternity. Then her fall was broken abruptly as her head made sharp contact with a rock and she screamed, the sound carrying her into a merciful oblivion.

The breath rasped painfully from her lungs as she lay within the shelter of the rocks. She had lost track of how long she had lain there. As yet she had made little attempt to move since to do so brought sharp reminders of her fall. Gently now she probed the bruises, then tried to sit up and felt the world tilt precariously. It was the rain settling on her face which finally roused her by its iciness. Shivering, she sat up waiting for the dizziness to return. Merci-fully it didn't come, though she felt strangely weak. Then realisation returned and with it dismay.

Unsteadily she got to her feet and stood for a moment before picking her way down to the shingle. Her hands felt the sharp contours of the rock as she edged her way along to the place where she had left the lantern hidden. It was not there.

Her heart contracted painfully. Numb with cold she fell to her knees, sobbing a little as she searched feverishly. Then her hand made contact with the metal object and she hugged it gratefully to her as she rose to her feet and began to make her way towards the shore-line. By now the sky was fully dark, the moon showing only intermittently between fast-moving clouds. She could hear the pounding of the sea against the shore and tried to hurry until caution returned.

Her eyes searched the darkness, but there was no sign of the ship. For a moment panic welled up then she shook herself mentally. They would scarcely make their presence known. She must get to the rendezvous and make the signal.

She was about to move when some slight sound held her. Her hands tightened against the rock. In vain she tried to pinpoint its direction and cause, then it came again and she sucked in her breath, feeling a chill of fear run through her. Someone was close. His feet had dislodged a shower of pebbles from the rain-soaked path where she had fallen earlier. Her nerves were taut so that she all but screamed as the figure moved, pausing for a moment as if he listened. It was something about his stance that drew the first chilling flicker of recognition from her. A shaft of moonlight broke suddenly from behind a cloud and in that instant she saw his features, the dark hair whipped against his head. He wore no coat, yet seemed oblivious to the cold as he moved, his booted feet grating over the rocks.

She crouched, hugging her arms about her body to still its violent trembling as Richard Kingston passed, so close that she was sure he must hear the pounding of her heart. But he did not stop. He moved on resolutely towards the cove. She rose stiffly, wincing at the pain of her cramped limbs, and watched with a sense of horror. There could no longer be any doubt, Richard Kingston was a spy and unless he was stopped would ruin the only chance England had of ever regaining its freedom from tyranny.

Her hand closed instinctively over the dagger. She pressed the other to her mouth to still the rising nausea and only then became aware of the tears which coursed down over her cheeks. She closed her eyes for a moment and opened them again, afraid to lose sight of her quarry. He was ahead of her now and she began to follow. There was no time to wonder whether she would be squeamish when it came to killing him. She had no choice. He had left her none. He was her enemy and must die rather than be allowed to betray all that she believed in.

It was only a matter of seconds before she realised that he was moving quickly; his boots finding far better footholds on the rain-drenched rocks and shingle than her own thin shoes could. She would lose him unless she could keep up. She began to quicken her pace, but within minutes knew that it was too late. She had indeed lost him. She paused, breathing hard, staring about her into the darkness. She tried to listen for some sound which might betray his presence, but the wind and the tide rising against the shingle obliterated everything. She bit her lip, uneasily aware that somehow she had herself become vulnerable. She was completely alone with no means of summoning help. Suddenly she had become the hunted rather than the hunter.

It was then that she saw the ship, its dark hulk becoming momentarily visible as the moon cast a pale light over the water. Her horrified gaze watched as it lay silhouetted against the sky, the men aboard deliberately putting their own lives at

risk. Somehow she must warn them, give them time
to get away before they could be tricked into coming ashore and walking into inevitable capture. But
how? She crouched against the rock. If she made no
signal they would return again the next night, and
the next, and sooner or later Charles Stuart would
walk straight into the trap. She shuddered, knowing that he would find no mercy at the hands of a
man as ruthless as Richard Kingston. He was like
the hawk who took his prey without remorse, and at
this very moment he watched and waited.

The hand coming suddenly down upon her
shoulder sent her whirling with terror, a scream
dying in her throat, crushed by the other hand
which closed brutally over her mouth. She struck
out wildly, only to be lifted as if she weighed no
more than a child. She fought desperately as arms
with the strength of steel imprisoned her. Struggling she was borne down. With a strangled cry she
tried to twist away only to feel the terrifying
strength of a body crushed down upon hers, stifling
her struggles, leaving her utterly defenceless. She
moaned, threshing feebly, turning her head from
side to side to avoid the face so close to her own.

'Be still,' the voice demanded. 'Be still and do
not scream or, by God, I shall have to silence you
and you'll not like the means I shall use.'

The scream died in her throat as the words penetrated her brain, leaving her numb with terror. Her
struggles ceased and she stared with angry, tear-
filled eyes at the face above her as Richard
Kingston said grimly, 'That's better. You are
learning.'

She moved beneath him, conscious of the
warmth of his body and of her own traitorous

awareness as the colour flooded into her cheeks. She turned her head, hating him afresh for the naked desire he could rouse within her. She sobbed as he held her relentlessly and heard his swift intake of breath.

'Damn you, why did you have to become involved? You give me no choice.'

Her eyes closed. He meant to kill her, then. Strangely, fear vanished. She had never expected mercy. He could not afford to let her live. Then something within her rebelled at so easy an acceptance of her fate. She still had the knife. Her fingers clawed desperately for it, closing over the cold metal. If only she could free her arm sufficiently to plunge the blade into his ribs.

She forced herself to relax, letting her body go limp as if she had fainted. He moved warily, releasing the pressure of his weight. It was enough, her hand rose, the knife flashed through the air as she swung it upwards then her eyes closed as she sobbed in terror. She could not do it. The blade caught his sleeve, tearing into the flesh beneath. For a moment he stared at the wound, then down at her, before his fingers closed savagely about her wrist, wrenching the dagger from her with an oath. He flung it away and she heard it clatter against a rock, but she was aware of nothing else except his anger and the blood coursing down his arm.

'You little fool,' he hissed.

She opened her mouth to scream, but he was too quick for her. Mercilessly he thrust her down, turning her struggling body until her face was pressed suffocatingly into the sand. A gag was forced into her mouth and within seconds her hands were bound. She watched helplessly as he rose to his feet and stared down at her. He swayed. It was only then that she realised she had wounded him more seriously than she had imagined. Strangely, the thought gave her little pleasure. Clutching at his arm he began to search for something and fresh horror swept over her as she guessed his intent. She struggled wildly, but it was no use. He had taken pains to see that she would not escape.

She fell back, trembling, as he moved to the water's edge. Through a blur of tears she watched as a light suddenly cut through the darkness, again and again. He was signalling the ship, setting his trap, and there was nothing she could do to prevent it.

Out of the night an answering light came within seconds. She heard him return, was aware of him towering above her before she was lifted roughly in his arms. And now he would kill her. She lay quietly as the warmth of his arms seemed to penetrate her body, draining her will to fight. A long, dark tunnel seemed to be opening up before her and as she fell into it she heard his voice. Ridiculously he seemed to be dragging her back, but it was too late.

CHAPTER
EIGHT

VOICES gradually penetrated her subconscious, intruding until she wanted to cry out in protest. A heaviness seemed to be holding her eyelids closed and when she tried to sit up it was to discover that the world was moving very oddly beneath her. She subsided again weakly and lay for a moment allowing the curious sensation to wash over her. Her mouth felt dry and she longed to ask for a drink, but every movement seemed to demand an effort of which she was incapable.

A desire to sleep surged over her again, but the voices would not allow it. Her eyelids flickered reluctantly open and she became aware of the figures, their features obscured by the glow of the lamp. It cast strange orange shadows across the face of the man who lifted his head. She heard him speak and felt an icy finger of fear thread its way down her spine as the familiar tones set her nerves throbbing. She lay unmoving, frozen with terror.

'I had no choice,' he was saying. 'She might have ruined everything. As it is, at least we can be sure of her silence until we have done what has to be done.'

'We had given you up,' the other replied softly. 'After we had put you ashore we kept the rendezvous each night, watching for your signal.'

'It's taking longer than we planned. Things have changed, there are more troops than we had counted on. I have not been able to make a move beyond a little careful reconnoitering of the area.'

Her vision cleared and her heart thudded as memory returned, bringing with it stark terror. She forced herself to feign unconsciousness while she listened and then became aware of the cause of the strange rocking movement. She was aboard the ship. Richard Kingston had brought her here and meant to keep her a prisoner while he sprang his trap.

Into the line of her vision stepped the man she recognised as Edward Wilmot. She saw his features beneath her half-closed lashes and had to prevent herself from crying out. Somehow she must warn him that the man to whom he now spoke was an enemy, yet the words seemed to stick in her throat.

The gag was gone from her mouth and, miraculously, her hands were also free. He must have been sure she would remain unconscious until he had had time to invent his story for being here. She tried to sit up, then moaned involuntarily, flinging a hand up to her brow as the world tilted yet again. But the sound was sufficient to rouse the men to action. She saw Richard Kingston's features harden as he turned sharply and moved towards her. She cried out, her voice hoarse with fright as she tried to ward him off.

'This man is a spy. He is a Roundhead and means to betray you.'

Her head swam as she struggled. Strong hands bore her down against the narrow bed. He meant to silence her. She flung a desperate glance at Edward Wilmot only to find, incredibly, that he was smiling.

'This is the man I warned you of,' she cried. 'He

has charge of the troopers. He has been watching your ship . . .' She was aware of the dark eyes staring down at her, of the hand gently brushing her cheek. Strangely, it was remorse she saw in his face as he murmured something softly.

It was some seconds before she realised that he had called her 'My dear love.' Her mind raced. Her senses reeled at his touch which was no longer cruel but surprisingly tender, so that for one moment she longed, crazily, to be gathered up into his arms. She moaned as the dream shattered.

'His name is Richard Kingston.' She twisted desperately away from him. 'He is a spy, a traitor. You must not believe what he has told you.'

She expected anger, a denial. Anything but the grim sadness she saw flood into his eyes. His face was ashen and she saw the lines of exhaustion etched into it now as he released her.

'You have every right to believe that what you say of me is true.'

Her teeth caught at her lip as she turned her head away into the pillow. 'I know you for what you are and I mean to stop you.'

Edward Wilmot came to stand at the side of the bunk where she lay. He held a glass of wine and raised her gently so that she could sip at it. Her hands shook and he watched, gravely, as she drank. She was aware of Richard Kingston moving away to stand with bowed head in the shadows, so that she could no longer see the expressions which flickered across his handsome face.

'You have been through a great deal,' Wilmot was saying, 'and you have been very brave.'

'I have done nothing. I wanted to warn you . . .' Her head jerked up, 'You must believe me.' Her glance was flung accusingly at the distant figure and she saw him flinch, yet he made no attempt to speak.

'There are things you have a right to know now,' Wilmot said, his own gaze resting on the other's face. For a moment she thought Richard Kingston meant to protest, but he was silenced, brusquely.

'She has a right to know. She is involved whether you like it or not.'

Her confused gaze went from one to the other as Richard Kingston muttered a violent oath and began to pace the small cabin.

'This is not what I wanted. You know how great the danger is.'

'Maybe so. But you said it yourself, we have no choice. Can we let her go now, believing as she does?'

Her mind raced. This was all like some great nightmare. 'I tell you, this man is a spy. Why do you listen to him?'

Wilmot's grey eyes narrowed, sadly. 'He is, as you say, Mistress Ashbourne, a spy. But not, as you believe, a Roundhead.'

She gasped. 'You are wrong. I tell you he commands the troop billeted at my grandfather's house.' The colour drained from her face. 'No man could do the things he has done . . .'

Wilmot shook his head, watching her closely. 'He has done what was necessary in order that people should believe him to be what he professes to be. It was no easy task.'

'Easy,' came the bitter retort from Richard Kingston, 'I have hated what I had to do.'

Her eyes widened and she was aware of his hands clenching and unclenching as he looked at her.

'Dear God, do you think I wished to use you or your kin as I have been forced to do?' he asked, savagely. 'You gave me no choice. I did what I could to try to prevent you from becoming involved.'

She shivered, remembering the violence of his assault upon her and as if he read her thoughts his mouth grew taut.

She longed to believe, yet every instinct warned her that this was all part of the trap. She stared at him through a blur of tears, shaking her head.

He had moved close but now came to a halt. 'It was never my intent to hurt you.'

She stared at him contemptuously. 'That day in the barn . . .'

'We were watched. I had no choice but to let it seem that the only thing I felt for you was contempt.'

Tears fell to her cheeks as she shook her head. 'You forget, I was present when Commissioner Thomas Thurloe spoke of Cromwell's eagerness for your return.'

'It is for the return of Richard Kingston that Master Cromwell yearns,' Wilmot said. 'The man you see here is not the same.'

She stared at them both, wide-eyed, her head aching with bewilderment.

'But . . . it cannot be possible.'

'Oh, it was not easy, there was a great deal of risk in substituting one man for another, particularly one so close to the Protector himself. It certainly would not have been possible had the real Kingston not been . . . shall we say detained, whilst engaged on some mission which took him from London to command a new troop in the South. Our timing had to be right and our informers correct in every detail. Even so, there has always been the risk that someone would know the real Kingston and put an end to our plan.'

She stared helplessly at the man who now seemed a total stranger. He studied her without moving, as if sensing yet her fear of him.

'I tried by every means I knew to keep you out of this.' His mouth quivered then, 'I never knew a more stubborn creature.'

She could find no similar humour in the situation. 'I might have betrayed you,' she whispered, and saw his brow raise slightly.

'That was why I needed your grandfather. He was my one ally.'

She stared incredulously. 'Your ally? I find it hard to believe. No one was ever more staunchly royalist, or so I thought . . .' Her voice trailed away as doubts intruded even upon those words. Nothing seemed to make sense any more.

'And I had good reason to thank God for it when he recognised me that first day,' he laughed.

She rose faintly from the bed and swayed a little. It was all too much to absorb at once. 'So that was why he tried to stop me.'

His arms held her and without thinking she leaned weakly against him, glad now of his strength. 'But what can you possibly hope to achieve?'

A glance passed between him and Wilmot and the latter shrugged. 'She knows enough. She has a right to the rest. In any case, there can be no going back now, for any of us.'

She looked questioningly up and saw the dark brows drawn together in a frown as he seemed to battle within himself. His hand brushed gently against her hair.

'I wished to keep you out of this. There are dangers you should not have to face and they are not yet over.'

Her head rose. 'I am not afraid. I know it has something to do with the King, this thing you are planning.'

He nodded, grimly, 'God willing, he will be carried safely to France, but all has not gone as planned. I was sent upon a special mission. I was to make contact with his friends and find a ship which would take him out of England. It was from that very mission that I was returning and rowing ashore when I had the misfortune to come upon a drowning girl.' His mouth twisted, wryly.

Her face was pale as she listened, her hands now in his. 'Why could you not simply have told me the truth?'

His mouth grew taut. 'At that time you were, to the best of my knowledge, a sympathiser of the Roundhead cause, and later . . . I longed to, but the dangers were and still are very great, and God knows,' his voice was low as he drew her close, 'I want nothing to happen to you.'

'All that matters is the King's safety,' she said defiantly, then stirred reluctantly in the warmth of his arms as she remembered something else. 'But there is Grandfather. He is old and frail and within a few days more troops will arrive at the house.'

'Which is why we have no time to lose,' he said grimly. 'It was our original intent to avoid contact once I was put ashore, until I had definite news of the King. But his failure to make any of the rendezvous has changed things. Something must have gone wrong. That was why I had to run the risk of contacting the ship tonight. We cannot afford any more delay. I shall have to risk going out to search for the King.'

She felt the wave of fear hit her. 'But how, where?'

'In any of the known safe houses. God knows, there are not many, but they are scattered.'

Wilmot frowned. 'Since Worcester, Cromwell's men have been scouring the country for him, and there is another problem—Captain Ennis is becoming restless, nor can I blame him. He puts his own life and those of his crew at risk and I doubt my ability to persuade him to remain much longer.'

'You must,' came the quick response. 'Somehow I shall get to the King myself and bring him here.'

'Richard, no!' The words were flung out even as she recognised the futility of them and her eyes filled with tears. He tilted her face up to his and she saw the look of wonderment in his eyes.

'Dare I believe that you care just a little what becomes of me?'

Colour flooded into her cheeks. 'It may be foolish to love when there may be no future for any of us,' she whispered, 'but if it is so, then I am very foolish.'

She heard his soft laugh of triumph before his lips claimed hers. It was a long kiss, full of tenderness, yet she sensed that it was only the presence of Edward Wilmot which made him hold back the passion she knew was waiting to be unleashed. Her body stirred in response until he moaned softly and put her quickly from him.

'Our future lies with the King. His safety is ours. It will not be easy, we must return to the house and

continue as if nothing had changed.' He released
her and dashed a hand across his brow. 'God knows
how I shall bear it to have you so close and not be
able to touch you. I wish there was some way I
could leave you here.'

She stared at him in alarm. 'I'll not stay without
you, in any case my disappearance would arouse
suspicion. A search would be made eventually and
someone would be bound to come to the cove. No,'
she said with a determination she was far from
feeling, 'I shall go back. I must.'

At that moment the Captain returned to the
cabin.

'The wind is rising, gentlemen. If you mean to go
ashore it had best be soon. I must get my ship away
from the rocks.'

'We are ready,' Richard said. 'Have the boat
ready.'

The Captain eyed Verity. 'Two passengers?'

Richard was already wrapping her cloak about
her shoulders and she shivered at its dampness.
'Yes, two.'

They left the cabin and climbed up on deck. The
wind had indeed risen yet, strangely, she no longer
felt afraid as she was lowered into the small craft
which rocked in the dark waters. Richard made to
climb the ladder after her. He paused at the rail to
speak with the Captain.

'Put off your departure for France as long as
possible,' he begged. Ennis stood, his hand gripping the rigging. 'I'll anchor here for three more
nights, as long as it's safe for me to do so. I cannot
say more. The King of France is my master and he'll
not thank me for jeopardising one of his ships, nor
for involving him in an English war. He risks too

much already by helping the Stuart.'

'I know it, and your help will not be forgotten.' He clasped the rigging and the proffered arm as he swung himself over the side, climbing easily into the small boat beside Verity.

All too soon they were ashore and climbing the cliff path. At the top they paused and Richard took her in his arms and kissed her. She could feel his muscular body straining against hers and she responded, her mouth burning beneath his, a sensation of fire surging through her body as he caressed her. Had he taken her then she would have offered no resistance and felt no shame at the thought. Yet it was he who drew away, putting her firmly from him.

'This is not the time.' He stared down at her, brushing the wind-swept hair from her face. 'Go now, quickly, before I forget what still has to be done.'

Weeping, she clasped her cloak about her and when she would have stayed he pushed her gently away.

'Go, quickly, or we may both be sorry.'

Through a blur of tears she took one last look at him before turning and running blindly towards the house.

An acrid smell of burning filled the air as she reached the courtyard. For the first time she remembered the fire. It all seemed such an age ago. She stood in the darkness, a hand pressed to her mouth as she stared at the sight that greeted her. All that remained of the barn was a charred shell. Troopers still carried water back and forth, but no longer with any sense of urgency.

Her gaze rose towards the glow of light at the windows of the house and she shivered as the rivulets of water soaked her shoes. From the shadows a voice came, sending her spinning round. With a gasp of relief she saw Thomas Rudd, his face rimed with sweat and smoke. He nodded towards the fire.

'It took hold fast. The whole winter feed stock is gone and nothing we could do to save it.'

She stared unemotionally at the ruins, 'I am grateful for what you did.' She turned to look at his shadowy figure in the darkness. 'You saw me return?'

'I was watching, but do not be afeared. No one else saw.'

'Has my aunt asked for me?'

His chuckle came to her softly. 'Not she. She was too afeared the wind might turn the fire towards the house and stables. But the Captain . . .' His voice fell, 'he saw you go and was away after you before I could stop him.' His eyes scanned the figures in the yard. 'He's not returned yet.'

She shivered in the icy air. 'We have no cause to fear Richard Kingston, Tom. He is our friend and at this moment he is in grave danger. We must help him. There is more at stake than you could ever dream.'

'Perhaps not so much, Mistress.'

She glanced up at him, surprised by the calm in his voice. 'You . . . know?'

He shrugged. 'I know he is not the man he claims to be, and if I know it, sooner or later some other will realise it too. It took some time, the memory has been rattling around in my head since he first came here.'

'You know his true name?'

He shook his head and she knew an instant disappointment. 'Nay, not that, but I have cause to know he is not who he claims for I once met the real Kingston. It was when he sequestered my dead brother's estates and left his wife and child without a roof over their heads.'

Her heart thudded as she looked at him. 'The pretence must go on a little longer.'

'You need have no fear I'll betray him. Whatever his cause, I'm his man.'

Her hand reached out impulsively to grasp his. 'Bless you. We may have need of you, and now I'd best get back.'

'Look to yourself,' he warned. 'Your cousin, Mistress Prudence, I've seen her wandering about the yard, and that one would be pleased to do harm to you.'

She nodded and felt a new sense of fear grip her. Gathering up her cloak she ran towards the house.

Making her way stealthily up the stairs she managed to reach the safety of her room and, tapping softly, heard Meg's voice answer.

'Let me in, quickly,' she whispered.

The key turned and she was admitted, closing the door quickly behind her. She leaned against it for a moment then moved to the fire. Suddenly her body was wracked by a shivering so violent that her teeth chattered. She was scarcely aware of Meg stripping the wet gown from her, or of the cup of hot broth she was made to drink.

'I'd given you up for lost,' the old woman muttered.

Verity nodded, her eyes already closing with exhaustion. 'How long have I been away?'

'Hours. 'Tis nearly dawn.'

Alarm flickered through her. 'So long?' Her hands shook as she held the cup. 'But I did what I had to do, that is what matters. Now it is in God's hands, and Richard Kingston's . . . or whoever he is.'

'Get into bed with you.' Meg drew back the covers and Verity slid between the sheets, feeling the old woman's hand linger against her brow for a moment.

'Aye, I thought so, you have a fever.'

It was true that her head burned and Meg's voice seemed to be coming to her dimly, as if from a great distance. She protested when she was roused roughly from sleep, to be raised from the pillows and some vile concoction poured between her lips. She choked, feeling the liquid sear at her insides, but Meg nodded.

'You'll be better by morning.'

Verity fought the veil of sleep which was descending again. 'Did anyone come searching for me?'

'Aye, Mistress Prudence, but I told her you were abed and that I had given you a sleeping draught and that nothing would waken you before morning, not if the house itself were ablaze.' She stared down at the still figure in the bed, seeing the golden hair spread across the pillows. 'And 'tis true,' she muttered, as she hobbled away to sit before the hearth.

CHAPTER
NINE

In spite of her exhaustion, from the moment her head touched the pillow that night, her brain had seemed infuriatingly to come alive. She had lain awake, tossing and turning, listening for some sound of Richard's return, until, with the dawn, she had finally fallen into a troubled sleep from which she had woken unrefreshed.

Her head throbbed as she dressed, and there were dark shadows beneath her eyes. She had always thought the grey gown unbecoming and now it seemed to emphasise her pallor. She smoothed back the tendrils of hair which escaped from her cap and straightened the folds of her white apron. For once her gaze lingered upon the image in the glass. How was it possible that her appearance should be so modest when, within, her head surged with new passions which threatened to consume her completely. Her eyes misted with tears. Somehow, for Richard's sake, she must behave normally, even though with every breath she longed for some sight of him, ached for the reassuring feel of his arms about her. She turned away quickly. Fate was too cruel. She was in love with a man who stood every chance of being killed and so much time had been wasted. Perhaps it was already too late.

Her stomach revolted at the sight of food and she sat staring at the piece of bread upon her plate as her aunt intoned grace. She made only a pretence of eating, crumbling the pieces between her fingers until her aunt reprimanded her sharply.

'Are you ill?' She frowned. In truth the girl did look unwell, but Harriet Ashbourne had little patience for any but her own bodily ills.

Verity dragged her gaze back from the window from which she could see the courtyard. 'No aunt. I still have a headache, that's all. Perhaps we shall have a storm.'

Her aunt's features were pinched and plain beneath the snood she wore. Beside it, Verity was aware of her cousin's gaze fixed rigidly upon her. Prudence was watching her every movement and she saw the pile of crumbs on her plate. She thrust it away, aware that she had betrayed her nervousness.

Prudence's eyes narrowed. 'I came to your room to rouse you last night when the fire broke out, but as usual you were not to be found when you were needed.'

Verity forced herself to meet her cousin's gaze. 'I had taken a sleeping draught, surely Margaret told you?'

'That old woman forgets her place.'

The dryness of her mouth made it almost impossible to form a smile as she spoke quietly. 'I'm afraid you are right, she is old and she still takes her duties seriously, in spite of the fact that I am no longer a child.'

Prudence's mouth tightened sullenly as she stared at her mother. 'It's time she went. She shows no respect and is a liability we can ill afford.'

Verity looked quickly at her aunt. 'That is untrue. She takes nothing save her food and a roof over her head. She has been with me since I was a babe. Surely out of that charity of which you so often speak, we should allow her to end her days in some comfort.'

Harriet Ashbourne's fingers strayed uneasily to the bible beside her. 'It is a miracle we did not all end our days last night. If the house had caught fire . . . We must say extra prayers in thanks for the Lord's goodness.'

'It was deliberate,' Prudence retorted, and Verity was aware of a pounding in her breast as she felt her cousin's gaze fixed on her suddenly.

'How can you believe that? One of the troopers or the servants may have been careless.'

Blue eyes narrowed. 'It was more than carelessness, cousin. I saw for myself where the fire began.'

'But who would wish to do such a thing?'

'Who indeed, cousin? I ask myself that very same question, just as I wonder that anyone could sleep through such noise and panic as was here last night.'

'I have explained . . .'

'So you have.' A frozen smile played about Prudence's lips.

'The sooner those extra troopers arrive the better,' Harriet Ashbourne said.

'I swear that my cousin would far rather see the house burned to the ground, mama.'

With the colour rising in her cheeks, Verity rose from her seat. She could sit no longer at the table without betraying her terror. Prudence suspected, perhaps not the truth yet, but something.

'If you will excuse me, aunt, I have no appetite.' She left the room, conscious of Prudence's narrowed gaze following her. Her cousin's curiosity might prove even more dangerous than the arrival of the troopers. Perhaps they had even less time than they had imagined.

Making her way to the kitchens she was only too pleased to busy herself with the tasks which were part of any household. There were always candles and soap to be made, gowns and linen to be laundered, fruit and meat to be preserved against the winter when supplies of fresh food would be unobtainable. But such activities whilst they kept her hands occupied left her mind free to wonder.

With her arms deep in the flour and the smell of fresh-baked bread in her nostrils, she wondered what manner of man Charles Stuart must be. To his enemies he was the devil incarnate and yet to those who followed him it seemed he could inspire so great a loyalty that they not only risked their own lives but would leave behind homes and possessions to follow him into exile. Such things did not reconcile with the image of a tyrant.

Her grandfather had spoken of him as 'tall as a giant and ugly as sin, yet having something about him which no woman could resist.' It was no secret that already he had his mistresses and even bastards. Her aunt spoke only of sin and carnal lust, and of the marriage bed in which a wife submitted to the needs of her husband in order to please, and to beget children. Such notions had filled Verity with horror, until now, when she thought of Richard, and the blush rose to her cheeks. If what she felt was a sign of wantonness then she was indeed wanton. She could not imagine lying inert and cold in his bed, or submitting with wifely duty to the needs of his body when her own desires matched his own so perfectly.

She emerged from the kitchens, stretching wearily in the cool atmosphere of the yard, when Richard appeared, mounted, at the head of his troop. For one moment their glances met and her heart leapt joyously. He was attired in the buff coat and breeches, a helmet crushed down over his hair, the breast-plate gleaming in the sunlight. She marvelled that such a sight would once have filled her with terror when now her entire being rejoiced.

His gaze seemed to burn into the very depths of her soul, yet beyond a tautening of his lips he gave no sign that he had even seen her. Her knees were trembling and she despised afresh the drab gown and the cap which seemed to rob her of the femininity of which he had made her so much aware. She watched until he was out of sight before turning reluctantly to the still room where she spent the noon infusing berries into the cordials and remedies which every household kept against a host of ills.

By the time the household was summoned for evening prayers, Richard had still not returned and she was restless with concern. She knelt beside her chair, hands clasped, head obediently bowed, but her aunt's voice faded as her own ears strained for a different sound and her heart became more and more uneasy. Why had he not returned? What if something should go wrong now?

Her head jerked upwards then as horses clattered into the yard. From where she knelt she could just see his tall figure at the head of the troop. She had to force herself to remain where she was—only then did the realisation come to her that there were still more troopers riding through the gates and she was sickened by the sudden implication. He

had returned and he had brought the reinforce-
ments with him.

She was jerked sharply back to reality as the great
bible closed with a thud and her eyes flew up to see
Prudence watching her with intent curiosity.

'So, cousin, the new troopers have arrived at last.
No wonder you look so pale. Now your precious
Charles Stuart will pay for his treason and his sup-
porters will be driven out of England. Very soon
there will be no place here for you or your kind.'

Before she could answer, Prudence had turned
and swept haughtily away and it was only as she
looked down that she realised that her hands had
been clenched so hard that the nails had cut into the
flesh and drawn blood.

She crossed quickly to the window, watching as
the buff-coated men dismounted and her mouth
compressed in terror as she saw their numbers.
What hope had Charles Stuart against so many?
She caught a brief glimpse of Richard as he strode
towards the stables. He had removed his helmet
and the rain had plastered his hair against his
head, leaving stubborn tendrils curled against his
neck.

It was as if she willed him to look up. He glanced
once, briefly, towards the house. She could not
even be certain that he had seen her and she dare
not risk giving any sign of her presence. With a sigh
she turned away. Why had those men had to arrive
now? One more day might have given them the
time they needed for the King to be got safely away,
but how was he to achieve it now?

She mounted the stairs and went into her grandfather's room. He was seated in a chair before the
fire and seemed to have been waiting for her. His

head tilted impatiently at the sound of her entry and he called out to her.

She went to him quickly, taking his outstretched hand. Jacob Reymes rose from his task of piling more logs onto the fire. His glance was troubled too, and only now did she fully realise that their agony must be every bit as great as her own.

She knelt before her grandfather's chair, seeing the candlelight enhance the greying hair and beard.

'Why did you not tell me?' she said, softly. 'If I had but known . . .'

He shook his head. 'What you did not know you could not be made to tell.'

'How could you believe I would ever betray . . .'

She was silenced as his hand tightened its grip. 'Believe me, child, there are men who know how to make even the most unwilling talk, and who care nothing for the means they use, nor whether it be upon a woman they use them.'

Tears sprang into her eyes. 'In my foolishness I put all our lives at risk.'

'Not foolishness, child, but ignorance, and the blame for that was as much mine.'

She swallowed hard. 'More troopers have arrived and there is still no word of the King.'

'Then something must have gone seriously amiss.'

'More likely Cromwell has every road sewn up too tight for him to risk moving out of hiding,' Jacob Reymes's voice cut across the crackling of the logs as he straightened up.

They started then as the door opened and a figure stepped quickly inside. Her cry of alarm became one of pleasure as she ran forward to be held in Richard's embrace and he kissed her gently before putting her from him to look to where the old man sat.

'Forgive me, Sir,' he said, quietly, and she saw her grandfather's brow rise.

'For what, young man? For loving my grand-child? She has royalist blood in her veins and there is none I would sooner see it mated to than a man of honour.'

She listened, her cheeks aflame as she stared up into Richard's face. His expression was grim.

'It is an ill time to be falling in love.'

'The times will get better,' with Reymes's help her grandfather rose unsteadily from his chair and stood with the aid of a stick. 'There may be years of exile ahead, both for the young King and for those who follow him. I ask your word that you will look to the safety of my grandchild.' She began to pro-test and was silenced. 'There can be no safety for her here once the King is gone.'

'Nor for any royalist.'

'I care not for myself,' came the firm response. 'But I would rather see your babes dead in their cradles than raised canting Puritans.'

She was aware of Richard's dark gaze as he stared down at her, his expression seeming to demand something of her. Her body trembled as he raised her chin and kissed her lips before he stared at the old man again.

'I give you my pledge, no sons of mine shall ever be raised in anything but loyalty to His Majesty, and my wife shall take her proper place at court, dressed as befits her, in satins and lace and none of this drab mockery.'

His gaze seemed to strip her of the gown, of her white cap and black silver-buckled shoes, leaving her mother-naked. She shivered, no longer in fear but in what seemed a wanton anticipation.

His brow darkened, 'But there will be no future for any of us unless we make a move, and soon.'

'It will be madness,' her grandfather spoke.

'It will be worse, Sir, to do nothing. The ship will sail without the King unless he can be brought here somehow.'

'And how is that to be done when every move we make is watched.'

Verity watched as Richard took a package of papers from his jacket. She saw a seal and her gaze rose uneasily as some premonition seemed to sweep over her.

'I have managed to make contact with a secret organisation who are working for the King's freedom.'

Her grandfather's eyes narrowed as he said softly, 'I know of them.'

'Indeed you should, Sir, since they are pledged to bring His Majesty back into his own again and you have been a member of that group these past months.'

Verity gasped, her senses reeling in confusion. Sir John shrugged, bitterly.

'I have done little.'

'Some day I will argue that with you, Sir. For now, I have news of the King's whereabouts and I must go to him with these letters. They give promise of safe refuge by the King of France and further pledge of gold and arms until such time as he is restored to his crown.'

'Then he must get to France,' the old man breathed.

'Yes, Sir. This is what he has been waiting for.

Now all that remains is for me to deliver it and him to safety.'

Verity started up, her eyes wide with fear. 'You may be killed.'

He drew her into his arms, his eyes narrowing with gentle humour. 'I have no intention of dying, my love. We have those fine sons to raise.'

She turned her face away, blushing, 'It is proper first to wed, Sir, and I have not yet said I will have you.'

His grip tightened, stirring within her a memory of those moments when he had been less gentle. 'Oh, you will have me, little one, even if I must first persuade you. But I warn you that the means I shall use will leave you little choice.' He kissed her then and she swayed weakly as he released her, the laughter in his eyes. His hand went under her chin, forcing her head up. 'Must I persuade you, my little mermaid?'

Her heart was beating uncomfortably fast as she shook her head and his arm went about her again. She looked at him in earnest then. 'Take Thomas Rudd with you. You need not fear,' as she saw him frown, 'he is to be trusted. His brother was killed at Naseby. He knows, has always known, that you are not the real Richard Kingston.' She frowned. 'Am I not to know, even now, your real identity?'

His hands cupped her face as he kissed her, his eyes serious. 'Better you do not. As for Thomas Rudd, I'll take him gladly and send word by him. I suspected from the first that he watched me a little too closely.'

'If he has guessed, then how many others . . . ?'

He put her from him and slowly gathered up his helmet and gloves. 'It is too late to think of that now. I must go to the King. Pray I can reach him in time.'

'God go with you,' she whispered as he left, and felt a shiver of fear run down her spine.

CHAPTER
TEN

IT was very early and she had escaped from the house and was in the garden gathering herbs when Thomas Rudd sought her out. She rose with a start and he put a finger to his lips in warning when she would have cried out. Gathering up the bunches of sage and rosemary she put them in her basket and carried it quickly to a shaded arbour where they would be hidden from the house.

She scanned his face anxiously. 'Is there any news? What of the King?'

'Aye, Mistress, the Captain has made contact with His Majesty and as I left him was taking him to a safe rendezvous.'

She released her breath joyfully at the news, 'Oh, thank God. Is the King well?'

His face grew taut. 'As well as any man can be who has been hunted like a fox these past weeks. He has been in hiding with the Wyndhams in Hampshire, but Cromwell's men were on the alert. Someone must have become suspicious and tipped them off, which is why he was not able to move.'

'And what is to happen now?'

He lowered his voice, warily. 'The King must have food and a little rest before he can be moved again.'

'But the ship . . .'

'It *must* wait. He is exhausted and in any event,

the Captain will make no attempt to move him until he can be sure it is safe.'

She frowned, but the argument was logical. 'Where are they hidden?'

'No great distance from here, but they are avoiding the houses. Those are the first places to be searched. There is a cottage, once used by a woodman but abandoned now.'

'I know it. But surely it is little more than a ruin?'

'Then less likely to arouse interest.'

She bit her lip, trying to imagine the King reduced to such state, and felt the tears prick at her eyes. She drew herself up. 'I will get food to them as soon as I can safely get away.'

'I'd go myself, but it would look suspicious if I were to be gone too long from my duties. Have a care though,' he warned. 'I passed troopers at the bridge and there is a lot of extra movement going on. They must suspect something.'

'Then all the more reason for the King to be moved as quickly as possible.' She glanced towards the house. 'You had best go now.'

Giving him time to return to the yard she followed, making her way towards the house. As she entered she saw Prudence, who called out sharply, 'Where have you been? Mama is looking for you.'

Verity held up the basket. 'I was collecting herbs.'

'Then take them to the kitchen, and be quick about it.'

Verity fled, aware as she did so that for some reason Prudence's glance had lingered upon her for just a little longer than usual, and a feeling of alarm stayed with her. Surely her cousin could not suspect? Nonetheless, somehow she must get away.

Her aunt had been watching for her and her temper was even more fractious than usual. To her dismay, Verity found herself obliged to remain under her watchful eye, carrying out her tasks, when every part of her being strained to escape. By the time she finally managed to get away, her arm was stinging from the blows she had received for her lack of attentiveness, but she no longer cared. Lifting the hem of her skirts she fled to her grandfather's room and was admitted quickly by Jacob Reymes.

'Is there news?' he whispered.

Nodding, she crossed to the bed and knelt beside it. Her grandfather woke, as if he had been waiting for her presence, and she saw the anxiety in his eyes.

'The King is safe,' she said, quickly. 'Richard is with him and soon, very soon now, will take him to the ship.'

'Praise be to God.' His mouth quivered, then she saw the fear which deepened the lines in his face. 'Child, you must let this matter rest now. You have done your part.'

She shook her head. 'How can I rest? The danger is not yet over. Richard needs help.'

His hand touched her cheek. 'You love him very much, do you not?'

'More than life itself,' she whispered. 'Which is why I must go, and I beg you not to try to dissuade me.'

He shook his head and she saw the grim set of his mouth. 'Would to God I had my strength.'

She bent to kiss him gently. 'I must go now, Grandfather. It will soon be over. Just a little longer. Surely nothing can go wrong now?'

She could but hope the words would prove true. It was not easy to leave him, knowing the torment he must be suffering, but now there was no time for delay. No matter what the risks, she had to get away from the house.

The pony whinnied in protest as she urged it on between the rows of trees. She could not blame it for its reticence, for the woods were full of shadows, the ground hardened by frost which still clung in webs of silver-grey sheen to the branches where the sun's rays had failed as yet to penetrate.

She rode cautiously, her breath fanning white into the air as she drew rein to listen. Her nerves were taut. It had been difficult to get away, with Prudence watching her every movement and with the troopers milling about the yard.

There had been more. Without Tom's warning she would have ridden straight towards them. As it was she had taken the longer route, cutting across fields, ignoring the risk that she might be stopped and questioned. Even then it was only by her own wits that she had managed to avoid a group of riders who came thundering along the road in the direction from which she had come. There had just been time to swing out of their path and dart back into a small thicket of trees from where she watched, sensing the urgency of their mission.

The men sweated beneath metal helmets and breastplates. The sun glinted on swords and flint-lock carbines. Their horses were lathered from being driven at so cruel a pace. But it was the man at their head who held her gaze and filled her with a new sense of urgency and foreboding as she recognised the hard features.

Not until the pounding hooves had faded away in the distance did she dare to move, and then it was to discover that she was trembling. The man she had just seen was known for his reputation as one of Cromwell's most dedicated followers. The net was closing in far more swiftly than any of them had imagined.

Digging her heels into the pony's flanks she rode, spurred on by desperation, feeling the chill air against her face. The path dipped and she slowed to manoeuvre a ditch. The pony stumbled, but managed to right itself. Bent low over the pony's neck she passed under low branches, leaving the path behind, then she straightened as her eyes finally found what they sought. Heart hammering she went slowly forward.

She dismounted quickly, hampered by the fullness of her skirts. Her cap was lost, leaving her hair tumbled about her shoulders, and her cheeks were flushed with the exertion of her ride. She made her way slowly forward. The cottage appeared deserted and she stared at it uncertainly. There was no sign of horses, nor of any presence, yet this must be the place. Tom had described it clearly and she had played here many times as a child.

She froze as a twig cracked, the sound reverberating through the still air. Even as some premonition warned her that she was not alone, she had the merest glimpse of something huge and hideous, descending from out of the heavens, blotting out everything before it enveloped her, sending her crashing to the leaf-strewn ground. Her scream was smothered by something heavy and suffocating. She fought wildly, lashing out with all her strength, and she heard a sharp groan as her fist made contact. That it was human offered no comfort as hands pinioned her arms, crushing her with a weight which all but knocked the life out of her, then a voice spoke with amazing calm in her ear.

'Whoever you are, be still, or I shall be obliged to render you senseless.'

A red haze of anger surged before her eyes and she writhed helplessly, aiming a kick which found its mark. The suffocating greyness was flung aside and she drew breath, turning her head. She gasped as pain exploded in a mass of brilliant stars. A scream died in her throat and as she fell into oblivion she was dimly aware of a sallow face staring down at her and a ludicrously large mouth suddenly contorted in horror, before blackness descended.

Her eyes flickered open and closed again as the world tilted painfully. Somewhere, very close, a voice spoke.

'Bring water, man, she's coming round.'

An arm raised her gently. A flask was held to her lips and she gasped as raw spirit burned down her throat. She thrust it away, fighting to the surface of consciousness. A cool, damp cloth was pressed against her jaw and she winced.

'Sire, allow me.'

Dimly she was aware that it was Richard's voice. Her hand rose to blot out the pain as she forced her eyes to open, then almost screamed as the face of her assailant loomed close. Strangely, those dark features were now filled with remorse and anger.

'God's death, man, let be. I've done many things in my life, but I've never injured a woman.'

'The blame is mine, for leaving you.'

Her mouth was too dry to speak, yet there were

so many questions she wanted to ask. Who was this stranger? Why did Richard address him with such reverence?

The blow had left her feeling weak and giddy and she struggled to rise, only to find that she was unable to do so. Richard's arm went about her and she rose unsteadily. For the first time she looked up into the stranger's face. He was dark, his hair, the eyes which stared at her so full of concern. His nose was too long, his mouth over-large, as everything about him, yet there was a sensuousness about him which sat ludicrously upon a man so ugly. He was tall, taller by a head even than Richard, and she felt a desire to laugh at the incongruity of a figure whose clothes appeared to be several sizes too small and whose lank hair had been so ill-cropped that it hung in jagged edges about his sallow features. Yet the laughter died on her lips and her heart pounded uncomfortably beneath her bodice. The heavy-lidded eyes regarded her now with an appreciation which brought the colour surging to her cheeks and the stranger smiled, miraculously transforming that ugliness to an indefinable charm.

'You might have warned me that you had a companion with you,' she said, hotly, stung to break the embarrassed silence. 'This . . . oaf near killed me.'

'I beg your forgiveness, Mistress Ashbourne.'

So he knew her name. She faced him as she clutched at the torn bodice of her gown, 'You are no gentleman, Sir.'

The dark gaze was lowered, but not before she caught the glint of amusement.

'I fear you are right.'

'Do you make a habit of leaping from trees upon your unsuspecting quarry, Sir?'

He regarded her solemnly and she saw some expression pass between himself and Richard before he answered, 'I confess to having acquired an affinity for them, Mistress. Particularly for English oak.'

She looked at his hands, so large and strong, and felt a strange uneasiness. Something about this man confused her. Beside that strength there was a softness. His appearance was that of a labourer, yet she sensed that he had never known physical toil. She saw Richard's mouth grow taut.

'The fault was mine. I should never have left you alone.'

To her amazement the other smiled, his manner unlike that of any servant she had ever seen. 'You have no cause to blame yourself. I should have stayed awake, but, alas, the need to sleep proved stronger than I.'

For the first time she became aware of the fine lines of exhaustion etched into his features and emotion stirred, mingling with confusion.

'Who . . . who are you?' She was aware of Richard's look of alarm and the stranger meeting her gaze directly.

'I very much fear we are discovered, James.'

Her glance flew upwards, her mouth opening in confusion. 'James?'

'My true name is unimportant,' the man she had known as Richard, was at her side, his face grim.

'Not to me, my lord,' a look of anger passed over the other's face. 'I shall have good reason to remember it for the rest of my life with gratitude.'

'I do not understand,' she whispered, and the stranger smiled.

'I owe my life to this man, Sir James Clifford. He

has performed many a service for which I, and England, can as yet only hope some day to be able to repay. But when that time comes, those services will not be forgotten. Some day things will be different. Order will be restored, and justice.'

She stared up at the tall figure. 'You speak as if you truly know such things, yet how can that be when only one man . . .' Her voice faded as the truth began to dawn upon her. Her knees trembled. 'S . . . Sire?' The colour deserted her face as she fell slowly to her knees. 'Your Majesty, can this be true?'

A hand reached down and she felt herself raised to stare into the gentle but frowning gaze. 'True indeed, Mistress Ashbourne, but better it were forgotten for the present.'

She struggled to find her voice. Thomas had warned her, but nothing had prepared her for this. It was inconceivable that the King of England could be reduced to such state. Dimly she was aware of Richard . . . James, for she must try to think of him thus, taking her hand and chafing it gently.

'Aye, true enough. But unless we get His Majesty to a place of safety until the ship can be ready, he'll not survive for long.'

Charles Stuart sat on a fallen tree stump, hands pressed against his knees to support his giant frame, and she was moved to compassion. Weariness was etched deep into the gaunt features yet he managed to force a smile.

'I am a troublesome burden. Perhaps it were better if they took me.'

James's face darkened grimly. 'Never say it, Sire. You have been through too much to give up now.'

'And what of my people, what of England? What

must they endure? My friends harbour me at risk to their own lives.'

'They do it gladly,' Verity spoke without thinking. 'You are their one hope. What right have you to speak of abandoning them?' She broke off, appalled by what she had said. 'Forgive me, Sire.'

'For what? You spoke the truth.' The King's gaze rose wearily to consider her for a long moment before he rose again to his feet. 'It is I who should beg forgiveness, Mistress Ashbourne.'

'Oh no,' she protested.

'Will you argue with me yet again?' A smile tugged briefly at the sensuous mouth and she could understand suddenly the charm of this man. 'I am tired. Cromwell's men hunt me like a dog in my own land. Can you believe, Mistress Ashbourne, that I have slept in holes so small that I had to lie bent double. I have even slept in a tree.'

In spite of herself she smiled. 'That I can believe, Sire. But why must you speak now of giving up when safety is so near?'

'Safety.' He brushed a hand against his brow and swayed slightly. A single stride took James to his side.

'You need rest, Sire.'

Verity started. 'I brought food, as you asked in your message. It is not a great deal. I dared not arouse suspicion.' She went to unfasten the saddlebag and took out a bundle. Charles Stuart's eyes rested on the chicken leg and the fresh-baked bread as he reached greedily for them and sank his teeth into the meat. They watched in silence until the first pangs of his hunger were sated and he looked up, shame-faced.

'You see, so soon I have forgotten the niceties. Is

this how you imagined your King, Mistress, tearing at his food like an animal?'

She spoke evenly. 'War makes animals of us all. You have the courage to win back your father's crown.'

He laughed grimly. 'It is far from won. If I leave these shores I go into exile.'

'Your friends are even now raising an army and gold,' James spoke beside her. 'You have but to give the word and they will follow your lead.'

The King nodded slowly. 'I am shamed yet again.'

'No, Sire. Any man who has suffered as you have done, must grieve a little. You need rest. A few hours is all I can pledge, but you shall have it whilst I stand guard. After that we must move. The Captain of the ship must be warned of our coming.'

Verity started. 'The troopers, I meant to warn you. More have arrived already at the house and I passed others on the road. There are sentries everywhere.'

'Damnation. Then we cannot stay here.'

The King swayed on his feet. 'If your concern is for me then it is needless. I've borne far worse than a night in the open. Another will not kill me.'

'By nightfall it will be near freezing and I dare not light a fire,' James reminded. 'Nor can I offer the protection you must have.' His brow furrowed. 'Someone must get to the ship and make the signal.'

Verity drew in her breath. 'Then I must go.'

'No.' James swung to face her. 'The danger is too great. The duty is mine.'

She shook her head. 'Your duty is here, with His Majesty. By nightfall these woods too will be crawling with troopers and if he is taken . . .'

'If I am taken then it is better I am taken alone,' Charles Stuart's voice broke in upon them, surprisingly calm. 'You have done enough. Leave me here and do what you must do. I will take my chances.'

'It is out of the question,' James's eyes glittered dangerously. Then, as if he remembered himself, he bowed slowly. 'No, Sire, Mistress Ashbourne is right, my place is here. The whole purpose of my mission is your safety. I know these woods and if it should come to it I can fight.'

'With a few hours sleep behind me, I might put up something of a struggle myself.' The King's eyes narrowed briefly in humour, only for it to fade again as it rested on Verity. 'But neither have I any taste for a woman putting her life in danger for me.'

She drew herself up. 'Someone must give the signal and the risk is far less for me, Sire.'

He scrutinised her intently and she returned the look. The privations he had suffered must have hit him twice as hard as most men. For his size alone he must have found it a constant torture to eat only scraps of food. His sunken cheeks gave evidence of it and her eyes strayed again to his hands. They were soft beneath the grime. He had not been born to hardship, yet he bore it with courage.

To her consternation he drew a ring from his finger and reached suddenly for her hand.

'It is my wish that you accept this small token. Some day I may hold it in my power to reward such loyalty as it deserves.'

She stared down at the jewel and shook her head. 'No, Sire, I beg you.'

His fingers merely tightened. 'It is little enough. Allow me this.'

'But . . . its value.'

'Purely sentimental, to me at least. It was the one thing I determined to keep, but it was given into the charge of Sir Edward Wilmot after we fled from Worcester and it became necessary for me to lose my identity.' He laughed grimly. 'Lose it? I feel I was never anything but what I am at this moment. The rest is all unreal.' He stared into her eyes for a moment, then smiled. 'This ring was returned to me by Sir James so that I should know from whom he came. It was given to me by my sister, Mary, before she left England to marry the Prince of Orange.'

'Then you should not be parted from it now, Sire,' Verity protested.

His hand tightened over hers. 'She would wish it, as I do. You see, we both know what it is to be forced to leave the home we love.'

She swallowed hard, her face pale as she nodded and would have made a curtsey. His hand retaining her grasp prevented it. He slid the ring onto her finger. It was too large, but he seemed satisfied and moved away to sit hunched against a tree.

James led her to her pony and as they stood, wrapped her cloak securely about her, his hands against her cheeks. She was almost afraid to look at him for fear she might break down, then, with a whispered oath and a glance at the distant figure, he swept her into an embrace, his lips scorching hers. She had no doubt but that had they been alone he would have carried her down onto the leaf-strewn ground and taken her. Her body ached with desire and she sobbed as he finally put her from him.

'God forgive me, but I wish I had taken you that day in the barn, even though it would have been rape and you would have despised me for it.'

Her hand rose to his mouth. 'Why didn't you?'

He shook his head, his face ashen. 'Because even then I loved you and knew that if I possessed you at all it could not be like that.'

'And I wanted you so,' she said, softly. 'I had to remind myself that you were my enemy.'

'Perhaps I am still as dangerous,' he said. 'I mean to have you. God willing we shall come out of this and then you'll not escape me again.'

Her green eyes flashed up to meet his. 'I shall not wish to escape.'

His mouth closed over hers then, savagely, he put her from him and swung her up into the saddle. 'Go now, woman.' She leaned against him, her hair falling in thick, lustrous waves over her shoulders. 'Signal the ship and tell Captain Ennis that his passenger will be ready tomorrow night. Today he needs rest. Warn Ennis to have a boat ready. We shall have to move quickly.'

She nodded. 'And afterwards? What of you? Your true identity will be known.'

His mouth tightened as he stepped back holding the bridle. Then, without answering, he released it, slapping the animal's flanks and she could only stare helplessly over her shoulder as she was borne away.

CHAPTER
ELEVEN

She sat stiff and straight in the high-backed chair as the man paced back and forth. Since her return to the house a kind of numbness seemed to have settled over her. Colonel Hastings's voice faded into insignificance as she watched the sun track a steady path across the polished floor, criss-crossed by the diamond panes of the window against which she sat.

The Colonel accepted a glass of wine and stood, back to the fire. He wore a blue coat under the steel breastplate, but it was the tawny-orange sash which denoted allegiance to Parliament which drew and held her gaze. He wore long bucket boots and had discarded the customary lobster-tail helmet for a wide-brimmed hat. That same uniform worn by the troopers she had so narrowly missed on the road. Her heart had all but failed her upon her return, to find them at Kingswood. An even crueller trick of fate had sent Colonel Hastings, the one man whose reputation for ruthless dedication to Parliament's cause was known across the length and breadth of England.

She clasped her hands rigidly in her lap, afraid lest they should betray her nervousness. His presence in this house could only make her own mission doubly hazardous, but there was no going back now.

He strode to the window to stare down into the

yard below where the seventy men in his command watered their horses, made repairs to harness and checked weapons. Verity allowed her gaze to linger as his attention was diverted. There was the mark of the bully about him in the thick neck and close-cropped grey hair. Everything about him bespoke strength and she did not doubt that he was a man who would use it to gain whatever he was determined upon. She sat, outwardly calm, whilst her heart thudded like some wild animal caught in a trap from which it knew there could be no escape. What had brought him to Kingswood now?

He turned suddenly, almost as if he sensed her fear and his curiosity was roused by it. He had watched her, surreptitiously, for some time and wondered at the nervousness she was trying so hard to conceal. He moved slowly across the room and stood beside her chair, seeing the immediate tensing of her hands. He smiled to himself then as it occurred to him that it was his male closeness which disturbed her. Though he fought for Parliament he had never allied his own beliefs to the fervour of the Puritans. He fought for a principle rather than for religious ideals and mistrusted the ruthlessness with which they shunned pleasure.

He moved purposely closer, standing so that he saw her eyes widen into startling pools of green, catching him unawares so that he drew in his breath sharply. She was a beauty under that drabness, he thought, and his gaze raked the plain, grey gown, sensing the body beneath, the softly curving breasts and slender waist. He felt lust tighten like a pain in his loins.

She trembled, as if he had actually reached out

and touched her, and he realised that he had been staring. The thought of having her, by force if necessary, excited him. He stood with one arm resting along the high back of her chair so that it brushed against the white cap she wore, and from which tendrils of golden hair escaped.

Unable to bear that closeness any longer, she rose involuntarily. She crossed the room, her skirts swaying about her ankles as she moved to the table and filled a fresh goblet with wine. The action obliged her to come close again and he took the wine, studying her above the edge of the glass with a look of amused speculation as she made no move to return to her seat. Her movements merely gave him an opportunity to study her more fully. The coarse gown she wore did nothing to flatter, but neither did it conceal the slender curves of her body. His knowing eye dressed her in something finer. The royalists at least knew how to dress their women to look like women and this one would look well in brilliant satins and lace. Or, better still, the thick lips twisted in silent conjecture, stripped of her clothes altogether.

As if she read the thoughts blazing in his eyes her face paled with terror. The danger he presented was far greater than she had imagined and she must keep her wits doubly about her. A few more hours and it would be dark. Her hands clenched fiercely. Nothing, *nothing* must prevent her keeping the rendezvous. Too much depended upon it for her to fail now.

Her aunt's voice brought her back with a start to the present.

'How can you be so certain, Colonel, that the quarry you seek is in these parts?'

He drained his glass, as if stirred from some deep ponderings of his own, before answering, 'We have our ways of knowing such things, Madam, and the little we do not know, we have means of finding out.'

Prudence made a pretence of sorting out some skeins of silk. 'I pray you capture Charles Stuart very soon, Colonel, and that those who aid him are punished for their wickedness.'

His gaze rested on the girl as she sat before the fire. 'You need not doubt it, Mistress.' She too wore a plain, grey gown, its sombreness relieved by white collar and cuffs, and from beneath its hem peeped one black shoe with its silver buckle. A pleasing enough picture, yet the Colonel was aware of an animosity which flickered between the two girls. Jealousy perhaps? The one with yellow hair had charms enough, but the real beauty was the girl whose icy rebuff had served only to intrigue him all the more. Hastings was a hunter and sensed a quarry. His narrowed gaze passed from one to the other and he became aware of the sudden pallor in the darker girl's face. It was fear he saw mirrored in the wide, green eyes. Naked, unadulterated fear, yet where was the cause?

'You will share our evening meal with us, Colonel?'

It was on his lips to refuse when he saw the golden head jerk upwards and something in the hunted look she cast in his direction made him alter that decision.

'It shall be my pleasure, Ma'am.' He leaned against the hearth, one booted foot crossed over the other, and smiled. 'A man grows tired of army life. I shall appreciate a few of the home comforts again.'

Numbed with despair, Verity knew that there was to be no escape just yet from this man.

Seated at the long table later that evening she merely toyed with her food. His presence had become almost a physical torture. As the shadows lengthened Meg came to light the candles, moving like a grey ghost about the room before taking her leave again. On a small table a clock ticked, driving the minutes before it like chaff in the wind, each more precious than the last. Verity felt her eyes drawn to it again and again and still Hastings sat, eating with relish everything put before him.

His chair was at the far end of the table, his face a dark, indistinct shape beyond the flickering circle of light. Purposely Verity kept her eyes lowered, but though she could not see him watching, she could sense it and felt a growing unease. Several times he addressed remarks directly to her so that she was obliged to answer and as he leaned forward the steel-grey gaze rested upon her.

'You are very quiet, Mistress Ashbourne. Perhaps our talk of the Stuart's capture distresses you?' He spoke quietly, leaning back in his chair so that once more she was denied seeing the expression in his eyes.

She dropped the crumbs of bread from her lifeless fingers onto the plate, her throat tightening. 'Distress me, Colonel? No indeed, why should it?'

'Because there are some who would be glad to see the Stuart back on the throne,' Prudence's voice intruded, sharply. 'Some who would do anything to bring it about.'

Hastings studied the meat on his plate. 'Such action would be most ill-advised. Rest assured

Mistress Ashbourne, that England will never return to the days when King rules both Parliament and Church.'

'And what has become of the Divine Right of Kings?' the words were out before she had even time to consider their foolishness and Verity was sickeningly aware of the speculative gleam in the Colonel's eyes as he set down his glass and regarded her intently. What devil had possessed her to say such a thing?

'The days are gone when we must endure the injustices of a King who was himself ruled by a Papist wife.'

She sat motionless as he stared at her through the rose-coloured liquid in his raised glass, and she knew that in those few unthinking words she had betrayed herself and added to his power. His thick lips tightened in triumph and she felt her flesh run cold, yet he sat, merely smiling, and the smile was suddenly in itself a threat.

Her hand fluttered faintly to her throat. 'Forgive me. I speak in ignorance. In truth I neither know anything of politics nor care.'

His eyes had narrowed to slits through which he watched her, keeping her features sharply framed within the range of his vision. She was lying and on the defensive, fighting almost for her life. The thought flickered through his mind that she was no Puritan after all, that he should call his men and arrest her for the undoubted royalist that she was. Wiser reflection warned there was more to be gained by subtlety. Give her free rein and like any wild filly she would run, and it would make the final capture so much more interesting.

He set the goblet down and rose to his feet. He

was over six feet tall and his shoulders broad as an ox.

'I had hoped to meet with Kingston.' He glanced sideways over his shoulder from the fire and the words struck yet another fear into her. Mercifully her aunt answered.

'The Captain rode out some hours ago. There have been reports, most of them false, of fugitives hiding in the area.'

'A man of Kingston's calibre would take no chances.'

Verity felt her hands tremble as she began to clear the dishes. 'You are acquainted with Captain Kingston, Colonel?'

The taper in his hand hung poised over a clay pipe. A cloud of smoke rose and he considered her through it. 'Our families are distant kin, his mother being some cousin or other to mine. The connection was slight I confess, until we rode together at Oxford. It is an acquaintance too long neglected. I look forward to renewing it.'

A dish fell sharply from her lifeless hands, crashing to the floor. As her aunt exclaimed angrily she knelt to retrieve the pieces, glad of any excuse to hide the anguish in her eyes. If James and this man came face to face then all was certainly lost. Somehow she must warn him.

It was with intense relief that she made her escape and sped to her room. She went at once to a table and drew up paper and ink, and without glancing up said, 'Margaret, somehow you must pass this message to Thomas Rudd. It is vital and no one must see.'

The old woman muttered unhappily, 'And where, pray, am I to be telling him to deliver it?'

'He will know.' She bit her lip, afraid of committing anything to paper, yet there was no other way. Finally she wrote simply. 'Hastings is here. He knows the real Kingston.' Sanding it she gave it to Margaret. 'Wait a while, until everyone is abed.'

'And where will you be?' The paper was thrust between her sagging breasts. She saw the girl's gaze fall and nodded. 'Aye, you may be right. If I know nothing there's nothing can be told. I'm old for playing games and old bones break easily.'

'I can tell you only that lives depend upon it.'

The woman bent and gathered up a cloak, but Verity shook her head. She crossed quickly to the oaken chest and began searching in it until her hand found the object she sought. She drew out a bundle of dark satin and shook it, holding the gown before her, conscious of Margaret's look of incredulity. With trembling hands she began to unfasten the grey gown she wore and stepped from it before she donned the other.

The moon was perverse, choosing this of all nights to spread its brilliance. Verity drew in shuddering breaths as she paused. In the pale light her features under the dark hood were wary, the wide-set green eyes anxious. Her escape from the house had been delayed by Colonel Hastings's reluctance to retire. She sensed in him a dangerous curiosity, but finally she had heard him take his leave, more drunk than sober.

The hour had already passed midnight as she drew her cloak over the gown and raised the hood over her head. Slipping from the house she had waited in the shadows until, satisfied that no one

stirred, she had run, urgency outweighing any feelings of caution.

Huddled against a sheltering rock she fumbled
with the lantern. Fear made her clumsy and the
wind had risen to buffet her skirts about her ankles
and whip her hair across her face. The gown with its
square neck appeared black in the darkness until a
shaft of moonlight revealed it as a deep green. The
skirts were parted at the front to show a rich under-
skirt of paler green embroidered with gold. From
the moment she had slipped into it her body had
responded to the feel of luxury against her skin
once more and she felt no pangs of guilt that she had
kept this one gown hidden from her aunt. She had
been startled by the image of herself in the glass, for
it had been like staring at a stranger. The colour lent
a vividness to her eyes so that they shone like
emeralds and her hair seemed a deeper gold, fram-
ing her pale face. She had hesitated over wearing it,
but it concealed her presence now far better than
the customary grey she wore, with its white collar
and cuffs.

The lantern flickered into life and she all but wept
with relief. Carefully she moved to the water's
edge, peering into the blackness. What if she was
too late and the Captain had given up his vigil? She
moved the lantern to and fro, its light cutting an arc
of brilliance into the night. No answering signal
came, no sound or movement beyond the crashing
of the waves at her feet. She was scarcely aware that
the sea soaked her shoes as she walked along the
line of shingle, desperately willing an answering
light to break through the darkness.

She dashed away tears, dragging wind-swept tendrils of hair from her face. Rain began to mingle

now with the spray, its blast lashing icily at her face, yet still she walked, reluctant even now to accept defeat. It was as she turned unwillingly to retrace her steps that she first heard the dull thud of oars and then saw, gliding towards her, the small rowing boat.

With a cry she ran forward to be held by the man who stepped ashore. Edward Wilmot took one look at her frozen features then drew her with an oath of concern into the warmth of his own cloak.

'Oh thank God,' she murmured, weakly. 'I feared I was too late.'

'We saw your signal, but made no answer lest it was a trap.'

'You were wise. There are more troops at the house under the command of Colonel Hastings.'

'Hastings?'

'You know him?'

'Aye,' came the soft reply. 'And that's enough.' He drew a small flask from beneath his cloak. 'Drink a little of this, it will warm you.'

She took it, obeying unthinkingly, and gasped as the fiery liquid burned her throat. But it did indeed fill her insides with warmth.

'What news of James?' he asked, grimly.

'He is with the King. I have sent him a warning not to make any attempt to return to the house.'

'Then at least the King is safe, God be praised.'

'Safe and well, though exhausted. He has suffered a great deal. I am to tell you that he will be here tomorrow night. A boat must be ready. There will be no second chance.'

'Never fear.' He moved closer then to tilt her face up to his and stared down at her. 'And what of you?

There is danger if you go back. Come to the ship with me now.'

For one glorious moment hope surged, only to fade as she shook her head. 'I cannot. Hastings already suspects that my sympathies are with the royalist cause. If I were to disappear now he would search even more ruthlessly.'

He released her and kissed her hand gently. 'Some day England will know how much is owed to your courage.'

She shook her head, her gaze rising anxiously to the scudding clouds above. 'I must get back, and you to your ship. I wish you and your precious cargo a safe journey.' Then, before he could reply, she had gathered up her skirts and began to run.

She climbed the cliff path in a state of dazed numbness, pausing for a moment to hug her cloak about her. Her own part was done. She had expected some sense of elation. A few hours more and the King would be safe in France with James by his side. Suddenly the tears were scalding down her cheeks, soaking the fabric of her gown. Edward Wilmot had spoken of courage. How could he know that she would need far greater courage now. The thought of defeat or capture was as nothing compared to the aching void in her heart as she thought of tomorrow when she would be alone again.

Her gaze had already picked out the first vein of grey dawn light in the sky and she began to walk, quickening her pace until the pain beneath her ribs was like a knife twisting at each step. She drew to a halt, pressing a hand to it as she looked about her. The trees were great moving shadows, the wind howling through their branches. It was like a human cry and she shivered, yet, incredibly, beneath the clinging dampness of her gown her body burned. She brushed a hand against her brow. A sense of weakness seemed to be consuming her. Her breath came painfully as she willed herself to go on. The house could not be far away now, but she looked about her with a dawning sense of apprehension. Suddenly she realised that she must have mistaken the path. Panic seized her and she turned, desperately, but each path looked the same, strewn with mouldering leaves. She was lost. Dizzily she began to retrace her steps, stumbling a little. It was then that she heard the sound and froze in terror. Horses, coming this way and close. Unthinkingly she began to run heedless of the briars which tore at her face and hands. But still the rider came closer and, suddenly, a cry.

'There. Seize her, don't let her escape.'

As if in a nightmare she heard the horse and rider crashing through the undergrowth, then they were before her, barring her path. She stumbled and cried out as hands dragged her roughly to her feet. A lantern was raised and she flung up a hand to shield her eyes.

'Aye, this is the girl.'

From behind the brilliance she was aware of a dark figure slowly dismounting and coming towards her. Her limbs trembled and she screamed as a hand suddenly held her chin and fingers twisted in her hair, savagely thrusting back her head.

She saw the gleam of triumph in Hastings's eyes and would have fallen in a faint had he not held her, jerking her upwards.

'What do you want with me?'

She heard his soft laughter, fighting to release her

arm, but his grip tightened and he was so close that his face was no more than inches from her own. 'There are some questions to be answered, Mistress Ashbourne.'

She fixed him with a defiant stare which belied the terror she felt. 'I have nothing to say.' She saw his mouth narrow mockingly. How much did he know?

'You wish to fight me?' He nodded. 'So be it, but if you have any hopes that I shall deal leniently because you are a woman, I fear you will be disappointed. I warn you, I have no qualms about using methods which, by very reason of your sex, you will find distressing. I may regret, just a little, making one so lovely suffer.' His hand held her chin so that she was forced to look at him and she was left in no doubt that he spoke the truth as his eyes narrowed cruelly. He was a man completely without mercy and she was in his power.

'I know nothing.' She saw him smile and realised that her defiance merely inflamed his desire for victory.

Out of the darkness another voice came then and she gasped with disbelief as Prudence stepped into the circle of light. Verity felt herself sag weakly, only to be held ruthlessly by her captor.

'She lies, Colonel,' Prudence cried, sharply. 'My cousin is a traitor. If you need further proof of it, I have it here.' She moved closer and triumphantly held out her hand. Verity gasped and jerked forward, but Hastings was too quick. Her arms were pinioned by one of his men as he took the object and held it towards the light.

'I fear you are betrayed, Mistress,' he drawled. 'This ring bears the Stuart cipher.'

'I found it in your room,' Prudence said, her face contorted with bitterness.

Hastings's features were suddenly cold. His hand rose sharply. 'Bring her.'

Before she could move Verity found herself seized and her wrists bound. Then she was lifted and thrust into the saddle of one of the waiting horses.

She had little impression of where they took her. There was a nightmarish quality about it all and only one thing seemed certain—Hastings meant his threat. She suffered no illusion that he would spare her any kind of torture in order to discover what she knew. He was aware that only she could lead him to the greatest prize in England and for how long would she be able to hold out against him? A few hours, that was all that was needed for James and the King to be away. Until then, no matter what the cost, she must tell him nothing.

She turned her head and met Hastings's glance resting upon her. Her blood ran cold. There was no escape and suddenly death seemed preferable to what this man intended.

CHAPTER
TWELVE

For some time she had taken no account of her surroundings but had simply sat upon the hard bed and stared at the locked door, feeling the panic surge over her. At any moment she had expected to see it open again and Hastings standing there. It was only as the minutes passed and then an hour that she realised that this was all part of the torture, that he was purposely leaving her alone so that she might have time to consider her situation and recognise her vulnerability. She should have known that Hastings was a man to resort to such subtleties.

After a while exhaustion had overtaken her and she had tried to sleep, only to find the cold jerking her to wakefulness again. She rose from the bed shivering, clasping her arms about her in a self-protective embrace. The one candle had spluttered and died long ago. She was surprised they had allowed her even that luxury until she had seen the shadows cast on the walls of her prison. Then she had sat huddled on the hard bed, afraid to blow out the tiny flame and thus plunge herself entirely into darkness, yet feeling her nerves stretched taut at every sound, every movement beyond the locked door.

On the table stood a pitcher of water. She poured a little. It tasted brackish but she drank greedily then stared about her. The only other furniture in the tiny room was a chair. She dragged it to the window and stood on it only to discover the frustration of finding it still beyond her reach.

From the pale sunlight now filtering down into the room she knew that it was daylight, but all sense of time was gone and she lapsed into fresh despair. She was not brave. How could she know that she would have the strength to defy Hastings?

The door opened and she shrank back as Hastings entered, closing the door softly behind him. He had abandoned his jacket and as he came to stand before her she was even more aware of his bull-like strength. He studied her in silence and she forced herself to return the stare, but he was not deceived. The green eyes mirrored her fear yet he sensed that she would not, even now, readily tell him what he wanted to know. The knowledge pleased him a little. He had merely guessed at the seductive charms which must lie beneath the dull, grey gown she had worn at their last encounter. Now, he found the reality even more enticing than he had dared to hope. She had discarded her cloak and he could see the creamy whiteness of her breasts and shoulders above the dark green satin.

A nerve pulsed beneath his thin, cropped hair as he moved to light a fresh candle, his hand shielding the flame. He studied her through the faint blue haze of smoke and smiled. Sooner or later she would tell him everything. He could wait . . .

Her gaze flickered to the door. Her eyes reminded him of a frightened doe.

'Where am I? What do you mean to do with me?'

His eyes narrowed. 'As to where,' he drawled, 'that is scarcely of consequence. The why however is a very different matter. I give you credit for some intelligence, Mistress Ashbourne.' His voice was suddenly hard. 'Let us not play games. We both know why you are here. You have knowledge of the whereabouts of the traitor Charles Stuart and his accomplice. I mean to discover it.' He paced the floor before her, his gaze never leaving her face. 'You have had time to consider. For your own sake I hope you have decided to be reasonable.'

There were shadows of exhaustion beneath her eyes, but she rose to her feet to meet his gaze and he felt a sneaking admiration for the manner in which, despite her fear, she feigned amused surprise.

'I told you, Colonel, I have nothing to say. I know nothing which could be of any interest to you.'

He sighed, regretfully, but said nothing. He drank a little wine from the flask he carried with him, aware that she watched his every movement with dazed intensity. Her hand trembled as she pressed it to her lips. She was thirsty and he could not blame her. Doubtless she was hungry too. With slow deliberation he wiped his lips and refastened the top of the flask. She said nothing, but he had seen the look in her eyes and knew that he must not make the mistake of underestimating her. She had pride and pride always took a little longer to break.

He leaned against the wall, one booted foot crossed over the other.

'I'm sorry. You are being foolish. Or perhaps you doubt my word that I shall use whatever means are necessary in order to make you tell me what I need to know.'

She passed her tongue over dry lips. No more than two strides separated her from Hastings. He had but to reach out a hand and she would be within his grasp. In her terror she could almost feel the thick, short fingers about her throat. Panic welled up. If only there was more air, or if she could see out of that solitary window. Her fingers fluttered to her throat.

'On the contrary, Colonel, I believe all that is said of you.'

'Then why put yourself to such torment, or me to the unpleasant necessity of having to inflict pain?'

Her green eyes narrowed. 'I doubt that a man like you finds such duty unpleasant.' She regretted the words instantly. It was foolish to antagonise him. 'I repeat, I know nothing. You are wasting your time.'

He straightened up slowly. 'I am in no hurry. I have all the time I need, so your stubbornness will avail you nothing.'

It was as much as she could do to stifle a laugh of triumph. For as long as he believed he had time there was hope. Too late she tried to lower the shutters over that gleam of hope in her eyes. He had seen it and was suddenly alert. His hand caught her wrist in a vice-like grip. His voice was low and threatening.

'I see I misjudge it, Mistress.' With a gasp of dismay she tried to twist away, but he held her too firmly. His face came terrifyingly close and she could feel his breath on her cheek. 'So, time, after all, is of the essence.'

'I do not know what you mean.'

His gaze narrowed, contemplatively, his fingers moving to twine roughly in her hair.

'It seems your memory needs refreshing, Mistress Ashbourne. I had hoped not to have to resort to this, but your stubbornness leaves me no choice.'

'What do you mean?' She stared at him.

He released her abruptly and strode to the door. She watched, heart thudding, then the breath caught in her throat in a gasp of horror as she stared at the figure standing, smiling, in the doorway.

'You!'

Prudence advanced, triumphantly, her blue eyes narrowed. 'I warned you, cousin, that some day you would regret having made an enemy of me. Well, the tide has turned at last. Soon I and England will be rid of your kind for ever, and I am glad, glad if I can help to bring it about.'

Verity shrank back, incredulous, before the malevolence she saw in her cousin's eyes. She searched desperately for some hint of charity, of pity, but there was none. Her cousin might have been a stranger.

'It was not my choice that we were never friends.'

Prudence advanced slowly, her face contorted with bitterness. 'Was it not, cousin? But then, you were never obliged to seek the charity of a roof over your head as I and my mother have had to do these past five years. Do you imagine it has been easy, watching you flaunt yourself as Mistress of my grandfather's house?'

Verity gasped, 'You know that is not true.' She staggered then, crying out as Prudence's hand came up and, before she realised her intent, had struck her across the face.

'Haughtiness will gain you nothing now, cousin. You forget, I can prove you the traitor you are.'

Verity watched, mesmerised, her hand clutched at her bruised cheek as she saw Prudence take a paper from her sleeve. Her eyes closed. There was something sickeningly familiar about that paper.

'Yes, you recognise it.'

Hastings moved closer. Verity shook her head in denial then moaned as his strong fingers caught and held her chin, ruthlessly forcing her to look up.

'Look at it, Mistress. Look well.'

She bit her lip in pain, trying to free herself, but his grip became all the more merciless. She tried to turn her head away. It was her letter. Her letter warning James.

'I don't know what you are talking about.'

'She is lying,' Prudence cried. 'Make her confess.'

Hastings's face was close and Verity felt the wave of nausea rise as she saw the look in his eyes.

'Oh she will talk, never fear.' He smiled then. 'I fear your little cousin has no love for you, Mistress.' He released her abruptly and she fell to the floor, sobbing with terror. She saw him snatch the letter from Prudence and read what was written there. In desperation she made a lunge for it, only to feel his boot send her reeling sharply back.

'So you tried to warn your lover. How very touching, and how very foolish.'

She brushed back the long strands of hair. 'What have you done with Meg? She had no part in this, no knowledge of what was in that letter.'

He laughed, softly. 'She is my prisoner. Your cousin did well to warn me of her suspicions.'

Tears misted her eyes even as her mind raced. With sickening dread she realised that her warning had never reached Richard, that he might still try to get to the house. Her eyes closed. Pray God he would remember his duty to the King. A few more hours, only a few.

Hastings's foot moved, viciously trapping her

wrist beneath his boot so that she screamed with pain.

'His name. The name of this traitor, Mistress Ashbourne? He must be of some consequence if you will risk so much to warn him.'

She heard Prudence's soft intake of breath, was dimly aware of her cousin watching her. Suddenly all prettiness was gone, transformed into a mask of bitterness as realisation began to dawn. She was staring in disbelief.

Verity shook her head, 'I will not tell you.'

Hastings's mouth tightened, grimly. 'This stubbornness will get you nowhere. You merely make matters harder for yourself.'

'I care not what you do to me.' She stared up at him, her face white. Suddenly she was dragged to her feet. His giant fist rose and she flinched, preparing herself for the blow, but strangely it did not come.

'Wait,' it was Prudence who spoke, her voice little more than a whisper. Verity saw the stricken look in her cousin's eyes as she moved closer. 'What a fool I have been. It can be only one man. I know who it is,' she hissed.

Verity shivered, her eyes pleading, but there was no mercy in Prudence's eyes. She should have expected none.

'I beg you,' she moaned softly, tears clinging to her lashes.

Hastings stood silent, watching.

'I must have been blind not to see it,' Prudence said. 'But you were clever, so very clever. This is yet one more example of your wickedness, cousin, and I shall be glad to see you pay for it.'

'His name,' Hastings rapped, impatiently at last.

Prudence's gaze was fixed upon her cousin's face, a tiny smile hovering about her lips. 'Kingston. His name is Richard Kingston.'

Verity saw the look of incredulity which flooded into Hastings's eyes. It vanished as he stared at her.

'Kingston? Are you mad?'

Prudence's blue eyes flashed, angrily. 'You think I could mistake it?'

Verity listened as she described James and Hastings's features hardened.

'It seems we have some deeper game here. No wonder you were so eager to warn him of my presence at Kingswood, Mistress.' His eyes raked Verity. 'Well, somehow we must see to it that he receives your message, though perhaps not this one.'

With a cry of dismay, Verity watched as he tore the note to pieces and let it fall. Prudence scuffed it viciously beneath her feet, tears of angry resentment misting her eyes. 'I am glad my suspicions of you proved right,' she said.

'I thought you were to be married,' Verity responded softly. 'You betray the man you love very lightly, cousin.'

Prudence made to fly at her again, but this time Hastings was too quick.

'Sheath your claws, my little kitten. There is time enough for that later. For the present my mission is of more importance than your own petty revenge. The question now is, if not Kingston then who is this spy?'

Verity met his gaze defiantly, her chin lifted. 'That at least is something I can never tell you, for I do not know.'

He considered her through narrowed eyes. 'I

believe in this instance you speak the truth. But we shall discover him soon enough, it is but a matter of time.'

'It is time we are wasting,' Prudence snapped. 'Make her tell you where he is hidden.'

'I mean to do so.'

Verity cried out then as he jerked her roughly towards him.

'We know that Charles Stuart is being hidden somewhere in this area.' He towered above her, his giant hands like claws of steel, bruising her flesh. 'He will not escape. My men are everywhere. When he makes his move we shall have him, and your lover too.'

Revulsion consumed her as he held her close, yet somehow she forced herself to speak, 'I can tell you nothing.'

Prudence uttered a cry of impatience. 'You are wasting time. There is another way.' Her gaze flickered over Verity, narrowing distastefully as she took in the fine gown, its decorativeness making a drab thing of her own.

'What do you mean?' Hastings asked.

'I mean what if the message were to be delivered in person?'

He frowned. 'Easier if we knew its intended destination.'

A smile touched her lips as she stared at Verity. 'We know it must be somewhere within this area. What if my cousin were to ride out, seemingly alone? Surely her appearance would bring the traitors from their hiding place?'

Hastings swore. 'Are you mad? You suggest we let her go?'

'On the contrary,' Prudence faced him. 'I am

suggesting that *I* go, wearing my cousin's gown.' Her hand caught at the satin and Verity backed away, her eyes wide with dismay as Prudence laughed softly. 'It will fit me well enough and with the hood of her cloak pulled over my hair, who will know the truth until it is too late. Your men can follow at a distance.'

'You could ride for hours in these woods and find no one.'

'But at least it is worth a try.' Her gaze flickered spitefully towards Verity. 'I know my cousin, Colonel. She is stubborn and even your persuasions may take time.'

Verity's heart thudded sickeningly. What if, by some cruel trick of fate, Prudence found the hiding place?

Her desperation must have shown for Hastings nodded. 'Try if you will. I can spare two of my men, no more. But I still believe my methods will bring the truth.'

'Your methods are your own concern, Colonel. I have no stomach to stand and watch. I shall want her gown.'

Verity gasped as Hastings's intent became clear. Her struggles were like those of a rabbit in the claws of a hawk as he held her, mercilessly stripping her of the gown whilst her cousin watched, unmoving. She was sobbing when finally he released her. With a brittle laugh Prudence caught the heavy satin as he flung it towards her. She paused at the door to look back.

'I shall bring your lover to you, cousin, in chains.'

Then she was gone, the door closing behind her and Hastings turned the key before his gaze concentrated upon Verity once more.

He stood in silence for a moment, watching her. 'You would do well to tell me what I want to know, Mistress Ashbourne.' His voice became suddenly softer and all the more terrifying. 'If you wish to save your lover's life you will tell me where he is hiding before my men can take him.'

Her gaze lifted contemptuously to his. 'So that you can kill him anyway?'

He moved, quick as a snake, to seize her. She tried to free herself of that cruel grip only to feel it tighten ruthlessly and she cried out as the breath seemed to be crushed out of her. Her senses swam as his face loomed above hers like some hideous mask. She tried to turn away, but his mouth came down on hers, brutally, his hands moving over her body, down her back, drawing her closer.

She screamed in terror, still held within the bear-like embrace, her hair swinging like a lustrous veil over his arm as her head fell back in a desperate attempt to avoid the terrible kisses. She prayed for oblivion then as she saw the expression in his eyes and knew that he had discovered the one sure means of gaining her submission. She sobbed wildly as he swung her from her feet and bore her, fighting, to the bed.

There was no way she could hold out against him, she knew it even as she fought with all her strength. Loathing and terror held her on the verge of fainting. He flung her down and his weight engulfed her, suffocating, so that she could scarcely breathe. His hands fumbled at her clothing, the strings of her cotton shift were wrenched apart and she screamed as his hands cupped her breasts and moved down towards her thighs.

Her teeth bit into her lip, drawing blood. The

more she fought the more impassioned he became. She heard his laughter and knew it to be all the more ominous for its apparent gentleness.

'You will tell me,' he said. 'Perhaps not yet, but very soon. I could almost wish I had time to prolong the persuasion but, alas, on this occasion I must forego the more exquisite delights.'

Her nails raked at his face, drawing blood. With an oath he caught her wrist, pinning it against the pillow, the close-cropped stubble of his hair brushing against her face.

She was suffocating. The room was spinning and she was helpless to fight off the hands which moved over her naked flesh. Tears scalded her cheeks as she fought, but his strength was too great. He was fumbling at his own clothing now then dragging her shift roughly aside. Her eyes had the brilliance of emeralds in the whiteness of her face, her hair was spread in wild disorder against the pillow. Hastings was too cunning to let her die as she prayed to do, yet, somehow she must gain time.

'No, for pity's sake. I will tell you,' she cried.

His face loomed grotesquely above her. For one moment he contemplated fulfilling his savage desire and taking her anyway. His body was afire, then sanity returned. Too much was at stake. With an oath he raised himself to stare down at her.

'I warn you, Mistress, I'll have no treachery. Lie to me and you'll pay more dearly than you had ever believed possible.' His fingers were at her throat, squeezing until she gasped.

'It is no trick. I will tell you.'

His eyes glinted dangerously as he watched her, realising that she found him repulsive, not merely for the methods he used, but as a man. His anger quickened, strengthened by the instinct that she meant to cheat him even now, yet a spark of admiration for her courage touched him.

'Speak then, and by God, it had best be the truth.'

She tried desperately to think coherently. Her voice came softly from her bruised throat. 'There is . . . a place. A house.'

'Where? Its name?'

She flung a hand across her dry mouth and felt the wetness of tears. His grip tightened again and she flinched.

'It is about a mile from here. Apsley Manor.'

A frown cut deep into his brow, but he moved and she moaned as his weight was suddenly shifted. He rose from the bed and stood watching her, incongruous in his state of half undress. Even now he could not be sure of her. It was possible she spoke the truth. He knew of Apsley Manor. It was, had been, a known royalist house until the Lord Protector had ordered its sequestration. Since then it had stood empty. A sound enough hiding place for desperate men.

She sat up, clutching the covers against her seminakedness. Pray God he would believe her and go and see for himself. Somehow she must get away and warn Richard, if that was possible. She would have to get to Thomas Rudd.

'What are you going to do?'

Hastings looked down at her, then reached for his breeches. 'I shall go and make a search of this . . . Apsley Manor, and you, Mistress, had better pray that I find what I am looking for.'

Hastings buttoned his clothing, shrugged himself into his coat and buckled on his sword. Then, to her utter dismay, he gathered up his cloak and flung it onto the bed.

'Put it on.'

She stared at it. Dear God, he meant to take her with him. Her gaze rose slowly. 'I have told you all I know. What more do you want with me?'

His mouth twisted cruelly. 'You take me for a fool. That is unwise.' In a swift movement he dragged her from the bed. 'You imagine I can be led on a wild-goose chase while you remain here? Oh no, Mistress.' She gasped with pain as he caught her and pinioned her wrists behind her with his own kerchief. 'We go to this house together, to see whether you are lying, and if so . . .' He laughed softly. 'Believe me, you will not make that same mistake again.'

Roughly he pushed her before him through the doorway. She blinked as sunlight hit her, then stumbled as he forced her towards the waiting horses. He barked out a command to his men and she realised that he meant to take her alone. Wryly she saw that he desired the glory of capturing Charles Stuart for himself.

She was lifted into the saddle and Hastings took the reins. It was a nightmare journey. Bruised and weak, several times she almost fell only to be jerked upright again. The trees were dense. Looking up through the thick foliage she tried to guess at the hour. It must be late noon, but soon they would be at the house and he would discover that she had tricked him and then, if as he threatened, he managed to make her talk . . . Would there have been time for Richard to get away with the King? Her breath caught in her throat and tears welled up.

Hastings drew to a halt suddenly and turned to

her. Bewildered she frowned. They were some distance yet from the house. Why had he stopped here? The answer came soon enough. She sat helplessly as he tore a strip from the hem of her shift and relentlessly thrust it into her mouth, securing the gag so that she was incapable of making a sound.

'Just in case you are telling the truth,' he sneered, 'I do not want you warning your royalist friends.'

Furious and helpless she was led forward until, in a clearing at the edge of the wood, he came to a halt again. There was no sign of movement. Hastings stared uneasily at the distant manor house, his glance rising from the shadowed lawns to the weathered red brick and the mullioned windows where a dying sun blazed like fire in the glass.

He dismounted, his hand hovering near his sword. He stood tense, alert. After a moment he came to her, dragging her from the saddle, and she winced as his fingers bit into the flesh of her arm.

'Let us discover whether you are truthful, or merely foolish, Mistress Ashbourne. I hope, for your sake, the former proves to be the case.'

The iciness of his tone struck fear into her. It was evident in her wide eyes as she stared at him. He drew his sword and, with the point, urged her towards the house. She moved reluctantly, her legs trembling. All she had gained was a little time, but at what cost? Her sidelong glance saw the anticipation in Hastings's eyes. No matter what happened now, at least she would have won this particular victory.

They moved across the grass, she in a state of terror, he warily, suspecting a trap. As they reached the house he caught her, his hand cruelly dragging at her hair as he drew her to a halt. Her head was bent back against his shoulder and he stared down at her.

'I begin to suspect that you were foolish after all. But we shall be sure,' he whispered.

His booted foot aimed a blow at the door. At the third blow it gave and she was pushed forward violently into a cold, half-light and the stench of neglect and decay. She shivered, still held as Hastings's gaze flicked over dust and cobwebs. Even to her own eyes it was apparent that no one had set foot here for a long time. She froze as he jerked the gag from her mouth and she licked her dry lips, longing for water. He stepped into the room. The great hearth still held grey ash and half-burned logs. With his sword Hastings shifted a child's doll from its place on the floor before he turned slowly and she shrank before the cold-blooded anger she saw in his eyes then.

She backed away, even as she did so, recognising the uselessness of the gesture. There was no escape. If she ran he would overtake her in two strides. She was bound and helpless and he was enraged by defeat at her hands.

'So.' The point of the sword rose and fell before her eyes and she watched it as if it were a snake about to strike. 'We come to the reckoning.' A sob of terror escaped her. 'What did you hope to gain?'

Perversely, desperation drove defiance into her gaze, catching him unawares and once again he found himself admiring her spirit.

'Time,' she spat the word in triumph. 'It is the one thing you lack.'

His eyes narrowed as he moved, uneasily, closer. 'Then if time is of the essence I must put to good use that which I have left, Mistress, for something tells

me that your precious lover has not yet won, or this
. . . farce would not have been necessary.'

She swayed, realising she had said too much.
'You are already too late.'

'We shall see.' There was a new note of menace in
his voice now. 'And this time we shall make certain
of the truth.'

Suddenly he was upon her. She was hurled to the
floor and fell with a sickening thud, unable to save
herself because of her bound hands. She knew
there could be no mercy for her now, when revenge
as well as desperation drove him. He would like to
kill her, she knew it, but to do it he must deny
himself the discovery of the information she still
held. She had already learned that, to a man like
Hastings, there was but one other way.

He moved towards her slowly, and her eyes
widened with stark terror.

She screamed as his hand reached out. He drew
her towards him, but he was in no hurry now. With
cold intent he dragged the cloak from her, then his
fingers moved to her shift, moving over the warm
nakedness of her flesh. She tried to move, but it was
useless. She was incapable of denying him, her
struggles were useless against him. She sobbed as
he lifted her then and carried her across the room.

His booted foot thrust open a door and, from the
corner of her eye she saw the bed, a great four-
poster, its hangings dulled by a coating of dust.

He flung her down and she gasped as the breath
was knocked from her. Hastings was unfastening
his jacket, his gaze never leaving her ashen face.
She was terrified, he could see it in her eyes, yet
even now he could not be sure she would tell him
what he needed to know. The fact made him more

ruthless. To be defeated by a mere girl . . .

He advanced towards her. With a cry she tried desperately to roll away from him, but he was too quick. He caught her, ruthlessly dragging her back until she lay beneath him, sobbing.

'I can tell you nothing, and even if I could, it is too late.' She prayed it was true as she said it.

His hand moved against her cheek, pushing back the long strands of hair.

'I trusted you once. You don't think you can escape me this time?' He moved, his weight crushing her. 'This can be as easy or as painful as you choose to make it,' he hissed, softly. 'And you may believe that I know of ways to make you talk such as you have never dreamed of.'

Her teeth caught in her lip. Her eyes were bright with tears, yet still she looked at him with defiance. His mouth closed upon hers and a cold wave of revulsion swept over her. She fought desperately, yet her struggles merely seemed to inflame him all the more. His lips moved against her neck, her breasts. His breath was hot upon her skin.

'I swear you are a witch,' he moaned. 'Who could blame a man for becoming enslaved.' Then he laughed softly. 'But I'll do what I must first, and take my pleasure afterwards.'

So he did not mean to let her go. Somehow her numbed brain absorbed the knowledge and hysteria drove her to desperate action. He had tossed his jacket on to the floor, then his belt, but first he had taken the pistol from it. Twisting her head she saw it where he had put it beneath the pillow. Her fingers clawed towards it, plucked it upwards and tried to turn it . . . to herself or to him? It no longer mattered. But even as she moved he saw her intent. With an oath he took her wrist in a vice-like grip, flinging it against the pillow above her head. The pistol fell, clattering to the floor, and she sobbed.

'That was foolish, Mistress,' he breathed. Holding her pinioned beneath him, he gazed at the unblemished exquisite perfection of her skin.

She had tried and failed. Her strength was gone. She was only half aware of a slight sound as a sudden movement came at the door. Half fainting she struggled to release herself from the crushing weight and heard Hastings swear. She cried out then as he groaned and sagged over her like a felled ox. Suddenly his hands had ceased their fumbling and she lay dazed, unable to move. Then she screamed, unable to shift him when, to her amazement, she felt his weight lifted and she was able to fill her lungs with air.

Opening her eyes she stared with disbelief into the anxious face of Thomas Rudd. He was bending over her, a hand behind her head as he poured spirit between her lips. As it burned into her she coughed and he straightened up, grunting with relief as he saw the colour flood into her cheeks.

'Thank God I found you. I feared I would be too late. Has he harmed you?'

She wanted to laugh with relief, yet tears coursed their way down her cheeks. She managed to shake her head as she sat up and held her hands out to him. Deftly he cut her bonds and she winced as blood began to throb through her veins again.

'How did you find me?' she asked.

His gaze rose from the prostrate form of Hastings. In a swift movement he removed the sword and pistol, tossing them onto the bed. 'I had been following you for some time, then I lost you somehow.'

She put her feet to the floor and rose unsteadily, supported by his hand.

'He was very careful.' Only now did she realise that she was trembling uncontrollably. Just one thought was in her mind now. 'I told him nothing, but we must get to James and the King. Hastings's men will be searching for them.'

He put the cloak about her shoulders. She swayed and he steadied her for a moment, then he smiled. 'Don't you fret, Mistress. They'll be safely on their way to the ship by now and we'd best be away ourselves.' She stayed him with a gasp as memory returned. 'My cousin. She took my gown hoping to find James and deceive him into thinking it was me. Two of Hastings's men were with her . . .'

To her surprise Thomas smiled. 'You'll not be needing to worry about Mistress Prudence. She'll not trouble us again for a while.'

'What do you mean?' Her dazed senses seemed unable to understand, but he made no attempt to answer, merely led her gently out to where the horses were tethered. Verity stopped in her tracks, then laughter bubbled from her lips as she stared at the sight before her. Prudence was seated upon her pony, but though her blue eyes flashed with rage and frustration, her mouth was prevented from giving voice to it by the kerchief which had been tied securely about it.

Her muffled screams of indignation increased as Verity moved closer. Her feet kicked savagely at the pony's flanks, but to no avail as Thomas held the reins firmly, checking the bonds which held her wrists to the saddle.

'But how . . . ?' Verity stared at him, pity for her cousin banished by the memory of what had happened.

He shrugged. 'I was following your tracks and stumbling around blindly, cursing myself for all kinds of a fool, when suddenly I saw you. It took me back a second or two, seeing you like that, or someone I took to be you. I suppose it made me a bit wary, at any rate I followed for a while at a distance.'

'But Hastings's men . . . ?'

He bent quickly to adjust the girths. 'Lying in a ditch. But that does not mean we're safe. We'd best get on, Mistress.'

She was trembling as he helped her into the saddle. 'What do you mean to do with my cousin?'

'We have no choice. We'll take her with us until we can be sure she can do no further mischief.'

Verity nodded. Only gradually was she beginning to realise that her ordeal had not been in vain after all. She had gained the time they needed, yet there were tears on her cheeks streaming unchecked as she rode. Exhaustion seemed to be flowing over her but she must not give way to it yet.

'I must get back to the house, to Grandfather.' And pray God, her mind raced on, there may yet be time to see James once more. She spurred the animal on, willing herself to stay in the saddle. To lose him now seemed too cruel, yet how could she regret anything if only it meant he was safe. Nothing else mattered. But her heart felt like a lead weight in her breast.

It seemed an eternity before they came within

sight of Kingswood. Darkness had come quickly as they rode, bringing with it a fine, chilling rain. With Thomas's help she scrambled from the saddle and made towards the house then stared with a feeling of unease up at the windows.

Turning to lift the squirming Prudence down, Thomas retained his hold on her as he moved to Verity's side. When she would have run up the steps and into the house he stayed her, frowning.

'I don't like it. Something's wrong.' He turned, staring across the empty yard, his gaze running from the charred ruins of the stable to the barn.

Verity shivered and drew her cloak more firmly about her. 'What is it?'

'I don't know, except that it is too quiet. Look about you. There are no horses, no men.'

'And no lights in the windows.' Verity's heart thudded. Even Prudence's struggles had ceased as she looked apprehensively about her.

Thomas removed the kerchief from her mouth, frowning. 'I suspect it will do you no good to scream, Mistress.' He released her wrists and she rubbed her bruised lips, resentfully.

'You will be sorry. Don't think you have won, and as for you,' her gaze went spitefully to Verity, 'it would seem your precious lover was merely using you and now he has fled without you.'

Biting back an answer, Verity evaded Thomas's attempts to restrain her and ran up the steps into the house, where she stopped, and drew in a deep breath. The hall was deserted. In the great hearth the fire had been left to die and the chill struck her forcibly as she moved slowly forward. With mounting terror she began to run to each apartment in turn, thrusting open the doors.

'Grandfather, Grandfather, where are you?'

With an oath Thomas reached her, quickly drawing her aside as, pistol in hand, he went before her. Gently he pushed her back against the wall, positioned himself to the side of the door, reached out to push it open and leapt forward. The pistol was lowered. He shook his head.

'This room is empty, as all the rest.'

Verity stared at him, her face stricken. 'Then where are Grandfather and Jacob Reymes?'

Prudence began to whimper where she stood in the centre of the hall, a pathetic figure now in the torn, satin gown, her yellow hair dishevelled.

'Where is mama?' She clutched her hands to her face and began to weep. Verity went to her, smoothing the damp hair from her cousin's brow.

'Hush, we will find her. We shall look together.'

Prudence pushed her away, her eyes wide with fear. 'Let me go. If she is harmed . . .'

'If she is harmed then it is none of our doing,' Verity tried to reason with her, but to no avail. To her dismay Prudence began to sob hysterically as she ran towards the stairs. Quickly they followed, then, with a gasp, Verity pointed towards the narrow glimmer of light which came from beneath her grandfather's door. She pushed it open and stopped, stunned, upon the threshold. The room was empty. A candle spluttered in its sconce. Automatically she moved to light a fresh one from the dying flame, her eyes taking in the room's disarray. As if in a trance she went slowly towards the stick which lay on the floor and she turned to Thomas Rudd.

'They have taken him. He could go nowhere without this. You know he could scarcely walk unaided.' Her voice was little more than a whisper.

He moved to the bed. Its covers were thrown back. He ran a hand grimly over the sheets. They were cold.

'It may not be as it seems,' he said, softly, but without conviction.

'Then what else?' Tears hung on her lashes as some memory nudged at her brain. She ran to the window, tugging aside the heavy curtains to run her fingers over the panelling. There was a click and a section sprang open. Quickly she delved inside then her hands froze upon the action.

'They are gone. Everything.' Thomas moved to her side. 'My mother's ring, he always kept it here. And gold, a velvet bag of coins. He said I must know where it was in time of need. There were papers too. Whoever it was, they must have forced him to show them this hiding place.'

Grimly, Thomas snapped the panel closed and drew her away.

'We must get out of here, before the troopers return. They must suspect someone may come here.'

She allowed herself to be led from the room, her brain too bemused to consider where he might be taking her.

A scream broke the eerie silence of the house and instinctively they began to run to where Prudence was tugging frantically at the lid of a heavy oaken chest. From inside it came muffled wails. Together they lifted the lid and Verity stared at the scarlet face of her aunt as she climbed, almost fainting, from her prison to fall into Prudence's arms. The two clung together, sobbing hysterically until, as if her aunt had suddenly become aware of her presence, she turned, her eyes blazing with anger upon Verity.

'You? What are you doing here? I thought they had taken you . . .'

'I am sorry to disappoint you, aunt,' she forced herself to speak. 'Where is my grandfather? What have they done with him?'

Her aunt's face contorted. 'You think I care? He is gone. They came and took him and I pray to God he never returns, traitor that he is.'

Blindly, Verity reached for Thomas Rudd's arm. 'We must find him. Where would they have taken him?' In a daze she began to run, scarcely conscious of the fact that he followed until he lifted her into the saddle and mounted his own horse beside her.

'What can you do against them, even should you find him?' he said, and she shook her head, neither knowing nor caring.

'I don't ask you to come with me. You have done enough. More than can ever be repaid.'

Savagely he dismissed that. 'We all fight for the same cause. I'll not desert you now.'

Mutely she thanked him, her eyes filling with tears. 'There is but one chance. I must get to James before the ship sails. There may yet be time. He may know what has happened, what can be done.'

'It is a slim chance, Mistress. It may have sailed hours ago,' he warned.

'Nevertheless, we must try. Have we any other choice?'

He said nothing, merely matched the pace of his own horse to her own, breaking into a gallop as she did so. She was exhausted, her mind in turmoil. Surely fate could not be so cruel. To lose the two people she loved most in the world was more than she could bear.

She was scarcely aware of the wind whipping at her skirts as she reached the cliff path, scrambling from the saddle without waiting for his help. A fine mist touched her face as she half ran, half fell towards the beach below, with no thought for possible danger. She ran towards the water's edge and stared out to sea, then her heart seemed to freeze in her breast as, in the far distance she saw it, the darkened shape against the sky, plunging with the waves which carried it away.

Helplessly she turned to look at Thomas and saw his mouth grow taut. She could not speak, but merely looked again at the waves lapping against the shore and felt the hot tears scald at her lashes.

'We are too late,' she whispered. 'They are gone.' Even now she could not believe it, her numbed senses refused to accept the evidence of her own eyes.

Thomas came to stand beside her, his own voice hoarse with emotion.

'Aye, Mistress, but the King is safe, God bless him, and we must be thankful for that. One day there may be better times for all of us because of it.'

There was no comfort in the words. How could there be when her own world had come to an end? She began to walk along the shore, her arms clasped about her body. Yet though she shivered she was not even aware of the cold.

It was over. He had gone from her life as he had come into it and a part of her own being had gone with him. He had had no choice, she knew that. His duty was to be at the King's side where he was needed. But what of her own need? How was she to fill the empty years ahead?

She no longer cared what happened to her. No pain could be worse than the pain she felt now. If she had only had time to tell him just once more of her love.

She was scarcely even aware of the sound behind her, assuming it to be Thomas who followed, until her name was called, softly. She came to a halt, listening, fighting the mists of confusion which seemed to have enveloped her brain. It was not Thomas's voice. She frowned. Her mind was playing tricks. She half turned, wanting to believe, yet afraid. It could not be . . . Every fibre of her being told her that it was impossible, even as she saw the figure moving towards her out of the darkness and she stared, her lips parted.

He spoke her name again and she cried out, launching herself into his arms, sobbing wildly.

'Oh James, James. I thought I was too late. That you were gone and I would never see you again.'

He held her to him, crushing her slender body against his, his mouth finding hers, then he cupped her face in his hands and smiled down at her.

'I am here. How could I go without the one thing in my life that has any meaning. I would have died first.'

She stared up at him, wiping the tears from her cheeks. 'But the King?'

He laughed. 'He is safe and on his way to France at this very moment.'

'But . . .' Her senses reeled. 'But he has need of you. Your place is with him. This war is not yet over, nor will be until he can return as King and claim his own again.'

He caressed her cheek, smiling. 'That day will

come. And I shall be with him. We both shall, in France.'

As if in a dream she shook her head. 'I do not understand.'

'You shall, my love,' he said, gently. 'The ship you saw was a decoy. The one carrying the King to France was hidden along the coast. I took him straight to it.'

'Then . . . how are you . . . we?'

'I have only to make a signal.' He left her and moved towards the rocks to return carrying a lantern. She watched in a daze as light flickered from it, cutting an arc into the darkness and within seconds an answering gleam came. She held her breath, releasing it slowly, then drew away from his embrace.

'But I cannot go with you. You forget, there is my grandfather. How can I leave him?'

He was smiling as he silenced her protests with a kiss. 'Did you think I would leave him behind? Jacob Reymes and I made plans from the first to get him to the ship. The King himself demanded it. You need not fear, he is even now bound for France, as we shall be before long.'

She allowed her head to rest against him, glad of his strength. 'Then it was you who went back to the house. But it was very cruel to imprison my aunt in the trunk.'

He laughed, softly. 'Not I, my sweet. True, we returned to the house for your grandfather. Your aunt saw us, screeched and fled as if the devil himself were at her heels. She put herself in the trunk. I merely decided to leave her where she was.'

Verity looked at him askance. 'But she might have died. The lid was too heavy for her to raise.'

He held her in his arms, smiling down at her. 'And you truly care what becomes of her?'

'I would not wish her harm,' she said when she was released from his kiss.

'No more did I, my sweet. I knew that someone would return. The servants or Mistress Prudence.' He released her, reluctantly, from his embrace some moments later when the small rowing boat was pulled up onto the shingle close by where Thomas was already waiting. Hand in hand they went towards it, and as she stepped aboard she laughed.

'The first time we met you put me ashore and I thought we should never meet again.'

His dark eyes stared lovingly down into hers as he murmured softly, 'But this time I take you with me and we shall never be parted again, my beloved little mermaid.'

Masquerade
Historical Romances

THE GOLDEN BRIDE
by Ann Edgeworth

When Lalia Darrencourt, heiress and acknowledged Victorian beauty, is jilted by her fiancé a week before her wedding she is convinced she wants nothing more to do with love, but when she discovers her mistake it is almost too late . . .

PRINCE OF DECEPTION
by Valentina Luellen

On her arrival in St Petersburg, Emma Fraser is horrified to find that the man she took to be a fellow servant is Prince Michael, head of the House of Adashev. How can she trust him when he has already deceived her once – especially when he seems to be so closely involved with the Czarina Catherine.

Mills & Boon

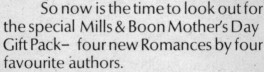

A lovely gift for Mother's Day

Mother's Day is just around the corner – on Sunday March 21st.

So now is the time to look out for the special Mills & Boon Mother's Day Gift Pack – four new Romances by four favourite authors.

The attractive Gift Pack costs no more than if you buy the four romances individually. It really is a lovely gift idea. You love Mills & Boon romances. So will your mother.

Point of No Return – *Carole Mortimer*
No Time for Love – *Kay Clifford*
Hostage to Dishonour – *Jessica Steele*
The Driftwood Beach – *Samantha Harvey*

Available in UK from February 12th. £3.00

Mills & Boon
the rose of romance